What the
Sword
Said
Steve Dixon

Other books in the *Rumours of the King* trilogy:
Out of the Shadows
The Empty Dragon (February 2004)

Scripture Union, 207–209 Queensway, Bletchley, Milton Keynes,
MK2 2EB, England.
Email: info@scriptureunion.org.uk
Website: www.scriptureunion.org.uk

Scripture Union Australia
Locked Bag 2, Central Coast Business Centre, NSW 2252
Website: www.su.org.au

Scripture Union USA
PO Box 987, Valley Forge, PA 19482
www.scriptureunion.org

British Library Cataloguing-in-Publication Data.
A catalogue record of this book is available from the British
Library.

Printed and bound in Great Britain by Creative Print and Design
(Wales) Ebbw Vale.

Cover: Hurlock Design

 Scripture Union is an international Christian charity working with
churches in more than 130 countries, providing resources to bring the
good news about Jesus Christ to children, young people and families and to
encourage them to develop spiritually through the Bible and prayer.
As well as our network of volunteers, staff and associates who run holidays,
church-based events and school Christian groups, we produce a wide range
of publications and support those who use our resources through training
programmes.

*FOR MY SONS
JACOB AND GABRIEL*

as they set off on their adventures

CHAPTER ONE

In his short life Ruel had never seen anything like this weather. Not that he could see much at the moment. The snow was driving into his face so hard that he had to keep his head down as he struggled on through drifts that were almost up to his knees. At thirteen, he couldn't remember many winters, but Zilla, the oldest of the adults who were with him, could remember more than fifty and she said it was the worst she'd known.

Ruel wondered how his friend Zilla was managing to keep going. He forced his head up and narrowed his eyes as the icy sting of the snowstorm lashed his face. He could just make her out, about twenty metres ahead and to the left. Normally her rainbow-coloured gown was the thing to recognise her by, but in this weather she was wrapped up in a thick woollen cloak, as they all were. And anyway the dull light turned everything that wasn't white to some shade of grey. It was late afternoon, but the light had been the same since early morning when they had set out from the mud huts of the village where they'd stayed the night before.

They were travelling in open moorland – nothing to see, not a rock or a tree or the slightest scrap of shelter – just rumpled blankets of snow on every side, disappearing into grey snow-filled mist. Visibility was poor, and it was vital not to lose sight of each other. Earlier, Zethar – the young hothead who seemed to have taken charge of the group – had tried to get the twelve of them marching in a column; but as the hours passed, exhaustion and disorientation had gradually made them lurch and stagger away from each other, and now they were scattered dangerously far apart.

Everyone's shape was the same in the snow-covered

cloaks but Ruel could identify them all by the way they moved. Zilla had a kind of rolling side-to-side movement and close by her was a figure who seemed to lever himself along with a stick that was as tall as him. That was Zabad. At fifty-four, he was the oldest man in the group and Zilla was even older than he was. Ruel made out another pair battling on against the storm, way up ahead. They were almost out of sight in the swirling snow but Ruel knew it would be Zethar and his friend Chilion, both with all the strength and determination of men in their twenties.

Another bunch of young men should be bringing up the rear. Ruel twisted his neck and looked behind, glad for a moment to take the wet hammering of the snow on the back of his head. Yes, he could make out a solid figure, leaning forward slightly, powering on without swaying to left or right like an ox pulling a plough. That was Thassi and behind him were the shadowy shapes of his four friends. That just left the sisters, Lexa and Rizpa, to account for. They were trudging an arm's reach away to his right. Lexa, the elder, planted every step with care but Rizpa, a teenager like Ruel, was stomping on as if she wanted to trample whoever was responsible for the storm deep beneath her sodden leather boots.

Having completed his check, Ruel let his chin drop to his chest and once again his world became a circle of snow, about two metres wide, directly in front of his plodding feet. He couldn't feel his feet. They were way beyond pain – just dead blocks that were carrying him along. His hands were completely numb, too, and there were icicles in his hair.

They had been travelling through snow like this each day for a week now, and there was no sign of any change. The first day the snow had started to fall had been like magic – huge flakes the size of butterflies, floating and drifting and turning the world into fairyland. They'd had snowball fights and even Zilla and Zabad had joined in. But that all seemed a hundred years ago now, and Ruel felt as if he'd be glad never to see another snowflake as long as he lived. He wondered how much longer he could carry on: which would break first – the weather or him?

The other possibility, of course, was that they'd get to the end of their journey. But the worst part of all they were going through was that they didn't know when or where their journey *would* end. Their instructions were simply: 'Go to the west of the Old Kingdom as far as you can, and meet me at the castle by the sea.' The problem was that they had no map of the Old Kingdom, and no one in any of the places they stopped could tell them more than the distance to the next village west.

The 'me' who'd given them these strange orders was Baladan, the slayer of The Dragon of Kiriath. Ruel and his friends had helped Baladan in his campaign against The Dragon, but he had left them soon after the adventure, telling them to wait in Kiriath until he sent for them. They'd waited from summer until the beginning of winter before word arrived. And when it did, they couldn't even be sure the message was *from* Baladan: it had come by word of mouth from a page-boy, who'd had it from a travelling beggar, who'd had it from a woodsman, who'd had it from who knew where. But the twelve friends had all been desperate to be doing *something*, so they'd set off in hope. That had been over a month ago, and here they were at the ending of the year, still travelling westward as far as they could tell, and with no idea how much further they had to go.

Ruel was starting to go off into a dream – pictures of the town of Kiriath formed in his mind, little scenes from the time they'd spent there. Then there were pictures of his home village of Hazar – the place most of the twelve friends came from – nestled away in the forest, west of Kiriath.

He was with his mother and father and his sister and little brother. It was summer and they were walking through the village together. Suddenly his sister grabbed his arm and shook him violently. Then all at once the summer picture disintegrated in a hail of snowflakes, and it wasn't his sister shaking his arm, it was Rizpa. He hauled his face up into the freezing blast, and saw that she was pointing ahead, where he could make out that Zethar and Chilion had stopped and were peering to their left.

Zethar turned towards them and cupped his hands round his mouth to shout. He had a powerful voice, but the swirling snow swallowed most of it and Ruel just caught one word struggling through the icy air.

'Lights!'

Slowly everyone struggled towards Zethar, gathering round him in a huddle.

'Where?' Zabad asked.

'Chilion saw them,' Zethar explained, and pointed off into the gloom.

Evening was coming now, and the greyness around them was on its way towards black. Everyone stared where Zethar was pointing. But no one could see a thing. Even Chilion couldn't see anything any more.

'You imagined it,' Thassi said at last.

They went on staring for a while longer without success, then Zethar set off walking again, and the others followed.

They kept together now, and everyone's heads sank again as they trudged on. Only Ruel forced his chin up, and screwed his eyes against the fierce snow that scoured his face, still staring in the direction they'd been looking. It seemed to him that the snow was easing up a bit and the mist was thinning. He desperately wanted to see lights. He *needed* to see lights. He knew they had to find shelter before dark or they'd die. Then suddenly he *did* see them.

For a moment he couldn't believe it. Surely it must be *his* imagination playing tricks now. But no, the lights didn't go away, and they didn't move about either – they were definitely there. Ruel tried to call out to the rest, but somehow it didn't work. His mouth moved, and no sound came. He took a huge breath, freezing his lungs, and bellowed. What came out was more like a strangled croak, but it was just enough for Rizpa to hear.

'Stop!' she yelled. 'Look!'

Once again everyone dragged their heads up to stare towards the horizon, and now they could all see the twinkling, surprisingly high up and far away to their left, almost like half a dozen stars low down in the dark sky. They let out a ragged cheer and wheeled to the left, striking out for the faintly glimmering hope of shelter. They were all bunched together and Ruel was right in the centre. He didn't look up again. He needed all his strength and will-power just to lift one foot after another. It was only the bodies around him that kept him upright and going in the right direction.

He managed to continue like this for about an hour barely awake, and then he stumbled badly, clutching the person in front. Luckily, it was the solid back of Thassi, and he didn't fall, but he was shaken into clear consciousness and he realised that he was staggering over stones. He focused for a moment and saw that they were on a rising pathway cut into solid rock. He forced himself to look up, and to his astonishment he saw the walls of a huge castle towering above them. Then a strange sound seemed to break around his head. It was like the roar and crash of waves. After that, he felt himself tumbling again, tumbling into blackness, and the tumbling didn't stop.

It was two days before Ruel was well enough to find out that the castle walls hadn't been a dream, and that the roaring and crashing hadn't been inside his head. He and his friends really *had* arrived at a castle by the sea, built on a huge rock. Salt water battered against three sides and the castle was certainly as far west as you could go in the Old Kingdom. It looked as if they'd finally reached their journey's end.

But there was no sign of Baladan. The wanderers had arrived just before the great feast of New Year but although the castle was buzzing with guests, as well as other snowbound travellers, Baladan was not amongst them and no one had seen him. Strangely, most of their fellow guests laughed when they were asked if they had come across him; and when Zabad went to the lord of the place, Earl Rakath, and asked after Baladan, the Earl acted as though Zabad was mad. He did, however, invite the friends to stay on into the New Year until the weather cleared.

And so, after weeks trudging half-starved through a snowy wilderness, the twelve ended up celebrating New Year's Eve in the Great Hall of a bustling castle, with fresh rushes under their feet, a roaring fire that made them sweat, and as much to eat and drink as they could manage. Earl Rakath and all his chief guests sat at a big table on a platform across the end of the hall. At right angles to this, long tables filled most of the room, each table packed with soldiers, stable boys, maidservants and manservants, clerks, carpenters, masons, and smiths – all the people who made up the community of a great castle. And at the bottom end of the hall were the travellers driven in by the winter weather. Ruel and his friends shared a table there with a group of cloth-traders bound for the north.

There was plenty of entertainment as well as good food to help them all welcome the New Year, and it was thanks to a song before the last course of their meal, that the friends found out why everyone seemed to know the name of Baladan but thought it ridiculous that anyone should ever meet him. A minstrel settled himself on a small platform just in front of Earl Rakath and introduced the song he was going to sing. He said that the start of a new year was a good time to look back over the last twelve months and that as one event stood out above all others as the most important of the past year, he'd written a song about it. With that, he showered notes from his harp and threw back his head.

'I sing of The Dragon of Kiriath,' he began, 'and its defeat by noble Baladan.' Everyone cheered and clapped.

What followed was the story of the mighty knight Baladan, mounted on a white horse the size of a small hill, swinging a sword the length of a castle flagpole and dressed in golden armour ten times brighter than the sun. The Dragon he'd killed had been so big it had stood over the town of Kiriath and kept the daylight off it for a year! Ruel and his friends were stunned. Then they heard their own names in the song. There was the witch Zilla who'd brewed up magic potions to weaken The Dragon, the boy Ruel who'd travelled to the ends of the earth to fetch Baladan to be their champion, and the heroic spy Zabad who'd led them to The Dragon's lair. By the end, all twelve of them had been mentioned – and nothing that was sung was anywhere near the truth of what they had done or what had happened.

There was a long roar of cheering and applause when he'd finished.

'If they think Baladan's like that, it's no wonder they don't think he's likely to turn up here,' Zilla said to Ruel. 'Heroes like that would have to live in a completely different world from us.'

'Have you any good potions on you, Zilla?' Rizpa butted in. 'I could do with something for my chilblains!'

Zilla gave her a sharp look. She wasn't pleased to have been called a witch.

But the traders at their table were obviously impressed with the minstrel's ballad.

'That's just how it was,' one of them said, as he passed the fruit.

'Exactly,' said another. 'I heard it all from a man who lives in Kiriath.'

'I met a friend of Ruel's uncle a couple of months ago,' a third one put in, handing round a bowl of nuts. 'He told me all the countries Ruel went to before he found Baladan.'

This was too much.

'I don't *have* an uncle,' Ruel interrupted.

'Excuse me?' the first trader asked.

'I *am* Ruel – Baladan's friend from the story – and I don't *have* an uncle,' Ruel told him. He felt furious, hearing his life – all their lives – stolen and twisted like that and he couldn't bear to let the story go unchallenged. 'And killing The Dragon was nothing like the way that man sang it in his song,' he went on. 'Baladan doesn't have golden armour. He doesn't wear armour at *all* or even look like a knight. And I didn't go to the ends of the earth to find him – I met him in the forest and I didn't even know who he *was*. *He* found *me* and came back to our village to help us. And this is Zilla.' Ruel pointed to his friend. 'And she's *not* a witch, she's just an old woman from our village that everyone thought was mad because she believed The Dragon could be beaten. And that's Zabad. He wasn't a spy – The Dragon made him collect its victims, that's all, until Baladan set him free.'

In a rush, Ruel went round the rest of them: Rizpa and Lexa, the sisters from the village of Maon that Baladan had saved from The Dragon, and the young men from Ruel's own village – Zethar, Chilion, Thassi and his four friends. Every one of them was just an ordinary person who had ended up following Baladan as he'd tracked down and killed a dragon that wasn't standing *over* the town of Kiriath but had disguised itself *inside* the town by stealing the shape of the local lord, Baron Azal.

There was an embarrassed pause after Ruel had finished.

'How long did you say you were out in the snow, son?' the first trader asked.

'It's nothing to *do* with the snow,' Ruel snapped back. 'What I told you is all *true*.'

'OK, son, if you say so,' the trader said, gently.

Zethar caught the patronising tone and leaned across the table.

'And what about if *I* say so?' he asked.

'What the boy says is true,' Chilion added. 'That song was rubbish.'

The second trader was out of his seat.

'We know what we know,' he said. 'The song's the truth. *Everybody* knows what happened at Kiriath. And if you've got anything else to say about it…'

He picked up the knife he'd been using to cut his food and pointed it at Chilion's chest. The other traders started rising from their bench, ready for a fight, and the young men from Hazar got up, too. Eyes locked, and it was just a question of who would make the first move when there was a deafening fanfare from a row of trumpeters and everything stopped. Earl Rakath was on his feet.

'Night is passing into morning,' he announced, in a great booming voice. 'The old year is passing into the new. The Dragon of Kiriath is dead. Perhaps it is possible, at last, that the power of the dragons in the Old Kingdom is passing too. Knights and ladies, squires, servants and every guest within these walls, I give you *the future*!' He raised his goblet and took a great gulp of wine.

'*The future*!' everyone roared.

On the first morning of the New Year, a blast from the horn at the castle gate announced a visitor. The drawbridge crashed down, the portcullis rattled up, and a mounted knight, covered in snow, clattered into the cobbled courtyard. It was clear even to Ruel, watching from one of the sheds built against the castle wall, that this was someone important. Squires came running, orders were shouted, and as the visitor's horse was led away to the stables, the castle Steward scurried down the steps from the Great Hall so fast that he slipped on the ice. He exchanged a few words with the new arrival, nodding and half-bowing all the time, then led him straight away to Earl Rakath's private rooms.

Half an hour later, a series of short clarion calls sent everyone hurrying in the direction of the Great Hall. When everyone was inside, trumpets sounded and Earl Rakath appeared with his new guest at his chamber door. The door was halfway up the side wall of the Great Hall, and stone steps led down from it to floor level but Earl Rakath stayed in his doorway where he could be seen. He was a big, broad man with a big, broad face which just then, had a big, broad smile all over it. His brown eyes were twinkling, and the dark curls of his hair seemed alive as he turned to right and left, taking in the whole crowd. Then he threw back his head and stretched out both his arms towards them all. Ruel thought he looked like one of the actors he'd seen perform in Kiriath town square.

'A challenge!' he boomed. 'A New Year's challenge to us all! What better gift for the New Year could there be?' He slapped his guest firmly on the back, which made him stagger and didn't seem to please him very much. 'Our noble friend brings word from Earl Melech, chief Earl of the

Old Kingdom, that he is to host a Grand Tournament in the autumn of the year.'

There was a buzz in the hall. Rakath let it run for a moment before raising his hand for silence.

'I know the autumn is far away,' he said, 'but so is Earl Melech's castle!'

A ripple of laughter ran through the hall. After a moment, he raised his right hand again and there was silence.

'Contestants are invited from every land in the Old Kingdom,' Rakath went on. 'Earls, barons, lords, knights, squires, common men – and women, too, if they wish! It will take until the autumn for such a mighty band of warriors to arm, train and travel from every corner of the Kingdom to Earl Melech's land.

'"But what is the purpose?" I hear you say. "What is the prize?" To find a Champion, of course! But this will be no ordinary Champion: this will be a Champion to lead a grand army – the army of all those who have gathered for the Tournament. But what is the army *for*? Who will it fight?'

He left a dramatic pause and scanned his audience for a moment before continuing.

'Why, none other than the dragons!' he said.

There were gasps and murmurings which took some time to quieten.

'Yes,' Rakath continued, at last. 'The dragons, and all the other monsters that infest our lands. The Kiriath Dragon is dead, and hope is alive again in the Old Kingdom. Earl Melech is calling us to rise and clear ourselves of the evils that have plagued us for longer than we care to remember!'

He punched the air with clenched fists and the crowd gave a rousing cheer.

As everyone was leaving the hall, Ruel caught a snatch of conversation between a carpenter and a blacksmith.

'Why bother? It's obvious who the Champion should be,' said the carpenter.

'Who?' asked the blacksmith.

'Baladan, of course!'

'If anyone can find him,' the blacksmith said with a laugh. 'Or if he exists!'

'Don't you believe the stories?' the carpenter asked, sounding rather shocked.

'What do I know?' the blacksmith went on. 'I'll tell you one thing for certain, though. This is going to mean plenty of work for me – Happy New Year!'

The blacksmith was right about the work. Before the day was over, orders were starting to flow in and he set about preparing the castle forge for prolonged action. Every knight would want a new sword and new armour, all of the latest design. All their squires would need equipping, and everyone else in the castle who wanted to take up the challenge would need a soldier's armour and weapons. It was going to take months to get everything ready.

But it wasn't just the blacksmith and his assistants who were busy. There was plenty for everyone else to do, too. Armour and weapons are only as good as the people inside them, so fighting skills would have to be practised, and old equipment could be used for that. As soon as he'd seen off Earl Melech's messenger, Earl Rakath set to work putting together a programme of New Year contests of his own. The snow had stopped falling, fortunately, and there was even a little weak sunshine as the flat ground to landward of the castle was cleared as a practice ground. Barriers went up around the cleared area and makeshift stands were built where the Earl and his noble guests could sit, wrapped in their thickest cloaks. Not long into the first week of the year, swords were clanging against armour, maces were crunching against shields, knights were being knocked off their horses, cracking their ribs, and everyone was having a wonderful time. In the middle of it all was Earl Rakath, red in the face from too much wine, his breath forming huge clouds in the cold air, roaring and cheering and telling everyone that these were the best New Year celebrations he'd had in his life.

Ruel and his friends were busy, too. Straight after the Tournament was announced, Zethar gathered them all together and said he thought they should practise for the competition with everyone else in the castle.

'If Baladan doesn't turn up, then we can still fight against the dragons,' he told them. 'And if he *does* come, we'll be ready trained to join him. He might not be the giant everyone seems to think he is, but he's sure to want to enter this Tournament and be Champion.'

Sometimes Zethar tried to push people further than they wanted to go, but this time he had no trouble persuading the other eleven. They'd come this far, and they certainly weren't going to hang around doing nothing then go home again.

He didn't have any trouble equipping them for battle either. They were all country village people, and none of them had weapons other than knives and clubs; but because so much new equipment was being ordered, plenty of old things were being scrapped. The friends all found work around the castle and, with the help of some hard bargaining from Zabad, Zethar soon got everyone all the equipment they needed – even Zilla and the sisters.

'Rakath was just making a joke when he said women could join in,' Chilion told them, then ducked when Zilla swung her second-hand sword at his head.

It was a wild swing. None of the friends had much skill with their weapons. But Earl Rakath had arranged training in the castle courtyard for people who weren't good enough to take part in the competitions outside, so the twelve joined in with that. Throughout the first couple of weeks of the New Year, they all lay down every night with aching muscles and bruised bodies from the hours of slashing and parrying, and the blows they hadn't managed to dodge.

One day, while the twelve were in the middle of a practice session in the courtyard, another messenger arrived. He provoked a different reaction from the one produced by Earl Melech's man. This second messenger looked like trouble the minute he rode over the drawbridge. He wore thick leather, rather than armour, and his head was uncovered, showing long tangled hair held back in a pigtail. He had a vicious-looking scar, running from forehead to chin, on the left side of his face. His horse was light and fast, not a knight's warhorse, and when the man brought it to a halt, it pawed restlessly, striking sparks from the cobbles. One of the gatehouse guards came to ask the man his business, but he never reached the end of his sentence. The man cut him off with a swipe from the back of his hand. He was wearing metal studded gauntlets, and the guard went reeling, blood running down his face. The messenger swung out of his saddle and made straight for the Great Hall, leaving his horse to canter round the courtyard, rearing and kicking out at anyone who came near it. Ten minutes later, he was back. He whistled once, vaulted into the saddle as his horse trotted up to him, and was gone.

There was a jousting match that afternoon at the practice ground, but Earl Rakath did not come to watch it and at the end of the day, he took his food in his room. It was the first mealtime since the twelve had arrived at his castle that he hadn't come to lord it over his high table. Ruel felt sure it must have something to do with the mystery visitor earlier in the day and, seeing the guard who'd been attacked sitting at one of the other tables, half his face raw and swollen, Ruel went to ask who the messenger had been.

'From Abaddon,' the guard mumbled. He was obviously in no state for further conversation, so Ruel went back to his friends. There had been a constant flow of travellers since the twelve had arrived and tonight they were sharing their table with a mixed group from different parts of the Old Kingdom. Ruel asked if any of them knew anything about someone or somewhere called Abaddon. Everyone stopped eating at the sound of the name and looked at him as if he'd just sworn.

'We know he's someone to steer clear of,' muttered a mousy little tin-smith.

'He puts ten days on my journey whenever I travel north,' said a trader in pots and jars. 'That's how long it takes to make a detour round his lands.'

'He's a robber chief,' a wool merchant explained. 'Works out of a castle right in the middle of the Kingdom. He's nothing but a jumped up swineherd's son but he rules the land around him like a lord. If you want to travel safely, you have to go miles out of your way to get past him.'

Mention of Abaddon seemed to spoil people's appetite for food or further talk, and it wasn't long before Ruel's table started to empty. Soon there was only one person left, apart from the twelve. He'd kept quiet all through the meal, and had hidden his face beneath a deep hood as he'd already eaten. Now that he was alone with the twelve, he slowly pulled back the hood and out of its shadows emerged a thin, sharp-featured face and a pair of deep, dark, piercing eyes

that were unmistakable. He smiled and nodded to them all.
It was Baladan.

chapter two

f the twelve were glad to see Baladan, the feeling didn't last long. Once the greetings were over, and they'd told him about their long journey, he explained that he had new orders to give them. Tomorrow, he said, they were to split up and set off in small groups, travelling in different directions across the Kingdom; they were to meet the adventures that came to them and keep going until they were told to come back. There was a surprised silence then Zethar explained about the Tournament, about the weapons they had collected and all the practise they'd done. He seemed sure that this news would change Baladan's plans, and his face shone with enthusiasm in the light of the torches burning along the walls of the Great Hall. Baladan heard him out politely then went on telling the friends which directions they'd be taking and who was to go with whom.

'Leave your weapons here,' he said. 'You'll find everything you need on the road.'

He didn't make any comment about the Tournament at all.

There were some strong words from Zethar, especially in the light of how they were being asked to team up.

'I say we stick with Earl Rakath and go to the Tournament with him,' he said.

This was open rebellion, and all eyes were on Baladan to see how he would deal with it. But he didn't react at all.

'If you want to get rid of the dragons, you have your orders,' he said. 'Whether you follow them or not is for you to decide.'

Then he left them alone to talk.

The discussion went on long into the night; but in the end everyone, even Zethar, decided to follow Baladan's instructions. After all, the orders might be strange, but Baladan had already defeated one dragon in a way that no one had expected. They went looking for Baladan to tell him what they'd agreed, but they couldn't find him. Next day, it was the same story. So in the cold wind of a January morning, they left their weapons with the castle armourer for safekeeping, and set off in groups on their separate ways.

Chilion's way was north. He had been sent out with just one travelling companion, and in the weeks that followed, he did not find this partner easy company. One morning in March, he found himself in what had become a familiar situation – calling out like a fool into what looked like an empty landscape.

'Ruel! Ruuuuuuuuel!' he yelled at the top of his voice.

A curved limestone cliff ahead cut off their route up the valley and the boy's name bounced back off it without any answer. The early spring sun had made Chilion sweat as he'd chased after his runaway partner along the valley bottom. But here, in the shade of the cliff, it was cold. Chilion shivered and scanned the shadowy arena made by the rock wall, searching for Ruel. The wide space was covered in stunted grass and heather and seemed quite open, but it was scattered with rocks and the occasional twisted tree and prickly bush. None of them looked large at a distance, but Chilion knew from experience that they were all big enough for Ruel to hide behind. The boy had put Chilion through this teasing game of 'hide and seek' almost daily throughout their journey together.

Water poured over the top of the cliff, gathering in a frothy pool at the bottom then flowing away down the valley. The pair had been following the winding stream since daybreak. A fallen tree trunk lay rotting beside the pool and Chilion marched up to it, kicked it, danced around with the pain in his toe, then collapsed onto it. He put his head in his hands and several times over, muttered all the swear words he knew. He knew quite a lot. Then he sniffed hard and realised there were tears pricking his eyes. They were tears of anger and frustration, as well as just plain misery.

Suddenly, something pinged off the top of his head. He looked up and another tiny missile stung his cheek. He saw it roll away into the stubbly grass at his feet – a sheep dropping. Sheep were the only living things he and Ruel had seen for days in this northern wasteland. A third round, black pellet hit him on the nose, then a shower of them landed all round him – Ruel must have thrown a handful. Then there was the boy himself, standing on a rock at the bottom of the cliff, laughing. It was hard, mocking laughter.

'How many times do I have to tell you?' Chilion shouted at him. 'How am I supposed to look after you if you keep running off like that?'

'And *I've* told *you* – I don't *need* looking after,' Ruel shouted back.

Their voices bounced off the rock wall like sling shots, making the place feel twice as cold and lonely as it was.

'Baladan said I had to look after you – *and* Zilla did.'

'Well, why didn't *they* come with me if they wanted me to be looked after, instead of sending me off with you? You're useless!'

Ruel slumped down on his rock with his back to Chilion.

Chilion turned away, too, and started ripping bits of bark from the tree trunk. Ruel and he must have had a hundred spats like this since Baladan had sent them off together from

Rakath's castle and each time, Chilion ended up feeling more and more of a failure. Chilion couldn't imagine why on earth Baladan had paired him up with Ruel. He had thought he'd be going with Zethar – they always did things together. And Ruel had obviously thought he'd be with his friend Zilla. But no. Chilion, who'd never looked after anything in his life before, had been sent off with a thirteen-year-old boy who didn't like him, and had been told to take care of the young wretch.

Chilion flung a handful of bark bits into the scrub. He closed his eyes and found himself picturing scenes from his village of Hazar. He was homesick – sick for the people of home. He saw his mother, leading their cow down the village street. She'd know what to do with Ruel. She always knew what to do. She'd only been a teenager when she'd had Chilion. His father had died not long afterwards. The Dragon had made one of his periodic calls for a sacrifice and when the lots were drawn, it was Chilion's father who had to go. His mother had picked herself up and just got on with things. She'd never remarried and had organised Chilion's life all by herself. Everyone said she was amazing. She'd even managed to get Chilion apprenticed to Machir the miller. Machir was someone else who always knew what he was doing. Chilion pictured the bad-tempered miller in the middle of a cloud of flour, barking out his orders for the day. Machir didn't suffer any nonsense from anyone. He'd soon sort Ruel out if he were here.

Then there was Chilion's friend, Zethar – wild, daring, always full of plans. More than anything, Chilion wished Zethar was with him to take a lead. But where *was* Zethar? That was the biggest mystery of all as far as Baladan's orders were concerned. Thassi had been sent out with his four friends, the rest had been divided into three pairs, but that meant one person was left over. That person was Zethar.

He'd been sent off on his own, and on top of that, he'd apparently not been told which direction to take. He had some secret quest that he couldn't tell anyone about – that was all that any of them knew.

Suddenly, Chilion's miserable thoughts were ripped apart by a shriek. He jerked round instinctively to look at Ruel, but even as he did so, he knew it wasn't the boy. It was a woman's voice. Ruel and Chilion scanned the area in confusion – the echo meant you couldn't tell where the sound had come from. Then it came again, splitting the air. And again – a sound of real fear. This time, they had it.

'Up there!' Ruel shouted, pointing above them.

No doubt about it – it was coming from the top of the rugged cliff which rose a hundred metres high in front of them. They stared at each other for a moment, then the scream came again and Ruel was off. The water cascading down the cliff had worn a broad channel into the rock and before Chilion could think, Ruel had reached it and was starting to shin his way up.

Now, at last, Chilion reacted.

'Stop!' he shouted, so forcefully that for once, Ruel did as he was told.

Chilion rushed to the bottom of the cliff and grabbed hold of Ruel's ankle, still just in reach.

'What are you doing?' the boy shouted down.

'You can't go up there,' Chilion told him.

'Why not?'

'You don't know what's at the top – anyway, you might fall – it's too dangerous.'

Ruel looked at him in disbelief.

'So what are we going to do?' he said. 'Just stay here and let her scream?'

Despite all the trouble he'd caused him, Chilion couldn't help admiring Ruel. As they stared at each other, it flashed through Chilion's mind that he was nearly twice as old as this boy but didn't have even half his courage.

'I'll go,' Chilion said, at last.

Ruel tugged to free his foot.

'Don't be stupid,' he said. '*You* can't do anything.'

'I said, *I'll* go!' Chilion repeated, with a fierceness which surprised them both. 'Baladan said *I* was the leader and that's what I've got to be. Now come down here or I'll drag you down! We're wasting time!'

A moment later, Ruel was back on the ground, watching Chilion inch his way up the rock wall with water spraying all around him.

Chilion was soaked in seconds. The water tumbling past him was freezing and his fingers went numb. The rock was wet, too, and worn smooth so that his hands and feet were slipping all over the place. There were a few little ledges and sloping bits to break up the climb but they were all covered in pebbles which gave way and sent him slithering. He lost count of the times he cracked his knees and elbows or scraped his shins. Two things kept him going – the screams still coming from up above him and the thought of Ruel down below, watching.

It took quite a long time but at last, Chilion realised he was nearing the top. He stopped to rest and as he clung there, he started to pick up another sound apart from the screams and the rush of water. It sounded like growling. He wondered if it could be something to do with the waterfall, but it definitely sounded alive – like some kind of huge guard dog. There was something else, too, coming through the fresh smell of the water – a hint of a filthy stench like a fouled-up stable.

He took a look above him, worked out where to put his hands and feet and set off for the top. A few moments later, he was crouched behind a rock perched right on the edge of the cliff. Moving a centimetre at a time, he shifted his head to the side and peered round the rock. One look was enough. He ducked back so quickly that he slipped and nearly fell over the cliff edge.

He huddled there, panting, trying to get a grip on himself and make sense of what he'd seen. About five metres ahead of him was a big boulder beside the stream which came over the cliff. On Chilion's side of the boulder were two people – a young woman and a strange armoured figure who, he supposed, was a knight. On the far side of the rock stood the thing making the growling noise and the stink. It was some sort of ogre – hairy, dressed in ragged animal skins and twice the size of a man. Chilion had registered, in the moment he had had to take in the scene, that the creature had been holding a rock over its head as if it meant to crush the couple like a pair of beetles.

But it didn't. The growling went on and so did the screaming. Taking as deep a breath as he could in the foul air, Chilion peered round the rock again. The scene seemed to be frozen. It was just the same as last time he looked. The ogre was still holding the rock over the couple but didn't seem to want to finish the job. Then, suddenly, it lumbered round and shambled away.

Oddly, the ogre looked as if it were trying to dance and was making weird little gasping noises which sounded something like laughter. About twenty metres away from the woman and the knight, it turned back towards them and started jigging on the spot, shaking the rock over its head and growling twice as hard. In a flash, Chilion realised what was happening – the ogre was teasing them. He watched as the young woman grabbed the knight's arm, trying to persuade him to make a run for it. But the moment they moved away from their boulder, the ogre took a jump towards them with a rumbling roar and sent them scuttling back. Then it just stood there, making its horrible gasping laugh.

Chilion hid behind his rock and cursed Baladan. All right, he couldn't have climbed the cliff in armour, but he could at least have carried a sword, slung across his back. Thanks to Baladan, he didn't have one, so how was he supposed to take on an ogre without any weapons? With his bare hands? Not likely! As he crouched behind the rock, an old familiar feeling started to creep over him. He hadn't a clue what to do.

'At least the couple are probably safe until the ogre gets bored with its game,' he thought. 'That might give me time to talk to Ruel and see what he thinks.' Slowly and carefully, he started to edge his way back down the cliff.

<hr />

Chilion didn't dare look below him so it was only when he was near the bottom that he realised Ruel wasn't alone. Above the sound of falling water, he could hear two voices in conversation. He twisted round to look, lost his grip and slithered the last couple of metres to land in a heap at the feet of the new arrival. It was Baladan.

Baladan hauled Chilion to his feet.

'What did you find?' he asked.

As quickly as he could, Chilion told them.

'What shall we do?' he asked.

To his surprise, Baladan just shrugged his shoulders.

'What do you suggest?' he asked.

Ruel was surprised, too. Chilion was the last person he'd ask for a suggestion about anything and he fully expected a 'don't know' from his companion. But Chilion had been working things out on his way back down.

'I don't think that pair can know there's a way down

the cliff,' he said. 'If we went back up and attracted their attention when the ogre had its back turned, they could probably beat it to the edge. And I bet the ogre's too clumsy to follow them down – it probably wouldn't even try.'

'Not bad,' said Baladan, looking up the cliff face. 'From what you've said, this "knight" might have a bit of trouble in his armour, but he might make it to that first ledge, and he could throw the stuff down from there. That might rescue the people – but what about the ogre? There's no ducking out – it'll have to be dealt with.'

Chilion was silent.

Baladan's horse, Hesed, was grazing, a little way away. His master went to him and unstrapped a long bundle hanging from the saddle. Ruel knew well enough what was in it. Whenever Baladan reached for his sword, it set Ruel's blood tingling. He remembered the first time he'd glimpsed it, when he'd first met Baladan – how the sunlight reflecting from a tiny bit of its hilt had seemed to set the world alight. Then there was the time that just a touch from it had healed an unhealable wound. It was hard to think of it as just a sword. Like Baladan himself, it seemed to hold secrets too deep to even think about.

Baladan unwrapped the bundle.

'Zethar said you'd all learned how to handle one of these,' he said, and he held out a beautifully decorated scabbard, half as long as Chilion himself. At its end, the golden hilt of the huge battle sword was glowing like a little sun in the shadow of the cliff. Chilion's mouth went dry and all he managed to do was nod. Between them, Baladan and Ruel adjusted the sword belt and positioned the weapon over Chilion's shoulder so that the blade hung down his back.

'Right, up you go!' Baladan told him, pointing at the cliff.

So once again, Chilion started to climb the slippery rock.

About ten metres up, he took a breather to work out his next moves and risked a quick look down. He'd expected Baladan, and probably Ruel, to be following him but he saw that they were both still on the ground.

'Aren't you coming?' he called.

Baladan's eyes locked on to his, and even at that distance, they seemed to have incredible power.

'*You* do it,' he said, and somehow, there was no arguing.

When he reached his hiding place at the top of the cliff, Chilion saw that nothing had changed. The sounds, the sights, the stink were the same. The couple must just have tried to make another break for it because the ogre was dancing towards them again. It came to a halt in front of their boulder and waved the big rock over its head, just as before. Chilion wondered how long this performance would go on if nothing were done about it. If the ogre hadn't finished off the couple by now, maybe it didn't intend to? Maybe it would get bored and eventually go away. Maybe all Chilion would have to do was simply sit there and wait. But then again, maybe when it became bored, the ogre would finish its game by crushing the pair. Baladan's words came into Chilion's mind: 'It'll have to be dealt with.'

As Chilion was chewing all this over, the ogre did its about-turn and started jigging away from the couple, wiggling its rear end at them. Chilion knew that it was now or never. He heaved himself onto his feet, marched up to the boulder, and when the ogre turned back to its victims, it found Chilion standing beside them, feet firmly planted, chest out, looking a lot more confident than he felt.

The creature gave a grunt of surprise but didn't charge. Strangely, it seemed rooted to the spot. Chilion reached over his left shoulder with both hands and gripped the hilt of Baladan's sword. The moment he touched it, he felt power surge through him: his heart raced, but not with fear – with pure energy. He gave a great shout, and pulled. The brilliant blade shot out of its sheath and the whole cliff-top was blasted with light.

Baladan and Ruel were there to help Chilion down the last few metres back to the valley bottom. Chilion eased the belt over his head and handed the sword back to its owner. He felt a deep sadness as he let it go, as if he were giving up a puzzle which he'd only half-fathomed.

'Have you cleaned it?' Baladan asked.

'No need,' Chilion replied. 'I never drew blood.'

He told them how, as soon as he had taken a step towards it, the ogre had whimpered and dropped its rock. Another step and the ogre started to shrink. By the time Chilion was halfway to it, it was the size of a dog, and when he was in striking distance, it was no bigger than a rat.

'It seemed cowardly to kill such a tiny thing,' Chilion explained.

'All the same, you *should* have killed it,' Baladan told him.

'If I could have caught it!' Chilion replied. 'Once I got near to it, it seemed to come alive and started running all over the place, squeaking like anything.'

Baladan laughed.

'Yes, they do move fast,' he said. 'And they turn up in the most unexpected places. It was a Dread. They feed on fear – that's what makes them grow. Courage shrinks them. Where is it now?'

'Probably miles away. It seemed to get its bearings then it shot away from us as fast as it could go.'

'What about the young woman and the knight?' Ruel asked.

Chilion explained that they hadn't wanted to come down with him into the valley. The route they'd been following was on the high ground beyond the cliff.

'That's where your route goes, too,' Baladan said. 'You need to follow them.'

So for the third time that day, Chilion braced himself for the climb.

'You lead,' Ruel said. 'You should be good at it by now.'

'I didn't think I was good for anything,' he replied.

The two looked at each other for a moment then Chilion began the climb. He was back at the top before he thought to check who was behind him. As before, he'd expected that Baladan would be following, but no. Ruel was with him this time but not Baladan. Ruel and Chilion stood on the cliff edge and searched the valley floor below for their leader. Not a sign. They turned round and could just make out the couple Chilion had rescued, halfway to the horizon. They set off after them.

Although they had a head start, it didn't take Ruel and Chilion long to catch up with the young woman and the knight, thanks to the knight's armour. He would definitely have had trouble making progress down the cliff with it on – he could hardly walk in it. Ruel and Chilion could hear it clanking long before they got up to the pair. That was *not* what a well-kept suit of armour was supposed to sound like. It sounded more like a cartload of junk on the move.

And that's what it turned out to be. The breastplate looked like an oven door, while the backplate was a drip-pan from the bottom of a roasting spit. The knight had a metal bowl on each shoulder and his arms and legs were stuffed into sections of lead piping, with tin saucers at the knees and elbows. A huge frying pan, minus the handle, hung from his left arm like a shield and on his head was a bucket with a slit hacked in it. The whole collection was held together with bits of string and there were knots and loose ends all over the place. The only thing that was real was his sword. It was rusty and had so many nicks in the edges that it looked more like a saw in places, but once upon a time it had clearly been a sword.

The knight made a long speech of thanks for Chilion's help, which was difficult to hear as he was still wearing his bucket. He introduced himself as Sir Shamma from the Land of the South, and when Chilion asked him what he was doing so far from home, he told them he was heading for the Grand Tournament at the Castle of Earl Melech.

'Have you come all the way on foot?' Ruel asked him.

The knight took off his bucket now, and Ruel was amazed to see a tangle of white hair and a face as wrinkled as old leather. He had to be at least as old as Zilla.

'Oh no, young sir,' he said. 'I have ridden the length of the Kingdom on the finest warhorse in the land but, alas, it was killed beneath me as I fought with twenty knights not two days ago. But I shall not be kept from the Tournament. I shall fight for the honour of being the Champion of the Kingdom if I have to crawl to the contest to do it! Even Abaddon shall not stand against me.'

'Abaddon?' Ruel asked, sharply. 'What do you know about him?'

He remembered the vicious messenger who'd caused such a stir at Rakath's castle and the effect the visit had had on its owner. Before the friends had left, the rumour was going round that Abaddon's messenger had made threats which had completely knocked the stuffing out of the boisterous Earl.

'I only know the name, young sir, only the name,'

Sir Shamma replied. 'It's the name on everyone's tongue. "Abaddon will be Champion": that's what everyone says.'

It appeared that Sir Shamma had been escorting the young woman, Ashti, to her home village when the ogre struck. So they all went there together. It was slow going, thanks to the old man's armour, but late that afternoon they came in sight of the village. As it was so late, Ashti invited them all to stay the night. Chilion and Ruel accepted straight away but Sir Shamma could not be persuaded.

'I shall not sleep beneath a roof again until I have lifted the Champion's crown,' he told them, and jamming his bucket back on his head, he clanked slowly on his way.

'What kept you?' Ashti's father asked, when they reached her cottage.

The young woman had been badly shaken by the encounter with the ogre and had been unable to speak for much of the journey home. Haltingly, and with Chilion's help, she explained to her father what had happened.

'If it hadn't been for Shamma,' she concluded, 'I might have been able to make a dash for it. I wish he'd stop wandering round on the roads and trying to escort everyone he bumps into.'

'He needs locking up!' her father said, roughly. He'd obviously been very worried.

'Do you know Sir Shamma?' Chilion asked.

'Sir, my backside!' said the father, and he stomped out of the cottage.

There was an embarrassed silence.

'He's not really a knight,' Ashti explained. 'They say one of his family *might* have been, long ago, but not him. He's just an old man who lives on his own between here and the next village.'

'No "Land of the South" then?' Chilion asked. 'No "warhorse" and "twenty knights"?'

'What do *you* think?' she said. 'We usually just play along with his stories. They're harmless enough but this Tournament is different. Ever since word of it got round, he's gone over the top. He never had that stupid armour before and now he's started this business of "escorting" people. It's an absolute nuisance, even if you don't run into trouble like we did today.'

'Why don't you just run away from him?' Ruel asked. 'He'd never catch you.'

'We have to stay with him to look after him,' she said. 'There's no way he can look after himself.'

⬥⬥⬥

Ruel liked Ashti. She reminded him of his sister, Safir, and later that evening, he found himself telling Ashti about her. Almost a year ago, Safir had been sent as a sacrifice to the Kiriath Dragon, and Ruel had set out to rescue her. With Baladan's help, she'd been saved, but then, only a few months later, Baladan had despatched him on this new mission and he'd had to leave his sister behind.

'I miss her,' Ruel said.

'She must mean an awful lot to you, for you to go chasing after a dragon for her.'

'She feels like half my life,' he replied.

He went on to tell Ashti how Safir was helping a knight, Sir Achbor, to manage his household in Kiriath. She seemed to spend most of her time with Sir Achbor and Ruel told Ashti that, in a way, he'd been starting to miss her even before he'd set out on this new adventure.

'It sounds as if she might be getting ready to be half of someone else's life,' Ashti said, gently. Ruel nodded and went quiet.

They'd been talking outside the cottage door and Ashti

went in to bed. It was a clear spring night so Ruel stayed out a bit longer, looking at the stars. Space. There seemed to be a lot of space in his life at the moment. No Safir. No Zilla. When he started thinking about Zilla, he kept getting mental pictures of 'Sir' Shamma. Zilla and Shamma seemed to be two of a kind – both old, both eccentric. It seemed obvious that if Shamma had ever been able to do anything with that battered old sword, he couldn't do it any more. His day was gone. And maybe so was Zilla's. Looking at the faraway stars, Ruel felt Safir and Zilla slipping away, out of his life – like smoke rising and disappearing into the sky. You couldn't hang on to smoke. It went through your fingers and was gone. Just now, all Ruel had in the world was Chilion. He felt very lonely.

Then he heard Chilion's voice. He'd been helping Ashti's father chop logs, and the two of them were walking back now, each with an armful of wood, talking easily, man-to-man, about nothing in particular. They nodded at Ruel as they passed, and Chilion smiled at him. Ruel thought he seemed taller, straighter in the back as he walked. Baladan's sword had hung down that back today. Chilion had drawn Baladan's sword and sent an ogre packing with it. Something of the glowing power of the sword still seemed to flicker inside the young man, lighting him up. It showed in his face. Ruel remembered throwing sheep droppings at Chilion that morning and felt sorry for it.

chapter three

uel and Chilion weren't the only members of the twelve whom Baladan had ordered north. Thassi and his four friends – Shual, Jaala, Hagab and Saraf – had been sent up the coastal route, and by late April, they'd gone about as far north as you could go in the Old Kingdom. In the past few days, villagers had been telling them that they were actually in the borderlands with the Northern Realm. The people they met would wave vaguely into the distance and talk about wild tribes and savage chieftains doing disgusting things to each other in the mist beyond the horizon. This made Thassi and his friends nervous – and nervous people become argumentative.

'It's all right for Lexa and Rizpa,' Jaala moaned, as they puffed their way up the slope of a heathery hillside. 'They got it easy compared to us.'

'You're not joking,' Hagab said. 'All they were told was to take a stroll along the south coast. It's probably been like a holiday for them.'

'And what about Zilla and Zabad?' Jaala went on. 'From what I made of their instructions, they'll end up not far from Hazar – but who knows *where* we're going to wind up?'

'At least we're not as badly off as Zethar,' Thassi reminded them. 'We're not on our own – and we know where we're going.'

'Do we?' Shual asked. 'What does "go north" mean? You seem to think it means "go on for *ever*", but Baladan never said we had to go *out* of the Kingdom, did he?'

'If we've come to the end of the Kingdom, it's obvious we ought to go back,' Saraf put in, stopping to get his breath back.

'We have to keep going till we get a message,' Thassi told them. 'That's what Baladan said.'

Baladan had also said that Thassi had to lead this group – and he wasn't finding it easy.

'Fine – let's go back to the last village and wait for a message,' Hagab suggested, pointing to the little dots in the distance which were the cottages they'd left that morning. 'You never know, if we wait long enough, we might hear some news of Ruel and Chilion. They must be getting near the border too by now.'

Jaala turned round immediately.

'Sounds good to me,' he said, and he took a step back down the slope.

'No, Jaala – hang on a minute!' Thassi called out.

Jaala took no notice.

'You wait as long as you want,' he shouted back. 'I'm going.'

'Me too,' said Hagab.

He took a step towards Jaala but a voice behind them brought him to a halt.

'You're going nowhere, my friend,' it said, in a harsh border accent.

They'd all turned to face Jaala and hadn't noticed the stranger ride out from the crags on top of the hill. They spun round to face him now. All except Jaala, who made as if he was going to run.

'I wouldn't do that, friend,' the stranger called out. 'I'll ride you down before you've gone ten paces.' He paused and sighed, as if slightly bored. 'And then I'll cut you to bits,' he added.

He drew his sword slowly and smiled. It was quite a short sword, with no decoration or shine to it, but it looked very businesslike. So did the man. He wore a breastplate but no other armour and he sat in the saddle as easily as if he spent his life there. His mount was more of a pony than a horse but it looked tough and sturdy, just like its rider. Jaala stopped.

'Good,' said the man. 'That was a bright move. Now – to business. You have a choice, friends: surrender – or end up as crow's meat. So what's it to be?'

His voice was friendly, as if he were offering a choice of food at a banquet, and he kept on smiling. He laid his sword flat across his saddle and it looked as if he'd be quite happy to wait for as long as it took them to decide.

'What's the hold up? Surrender!' Saraf hissed to Thassi.

'We can't fight him – we've no weapons,' Shual said.

'Thanks to Baladan,' Hagab muttered.

Jaala had rejoined them and he was for surrendering, too. So that's what they did. Thassi knew, and his friends knew, that although they called him their leader, he wasn't going to stand against them. That's the way it had been throughout the four months of their journey.

'You made a good choice,' the man told them. 'Now, what happens next is that I need to see your money.'

'We haven't got any,' Thassi said.

'Really? Well, we'll just check that out, shall we? Sit yourselves down, friends, and if you wouldn't mind, just come over to me one at a time.'

The man jumped off his pony, sheathed his sword, and as the friends came over to him one by one, he searched them. He was efficient and thorough and it was over very quickly.

'Well!' he said, when he'd finished. 'You really *don't* have any money. Or any food. You must be starving. Come with me.' He led them up to the crags which made a natural wall round the top of the hill. 'Quite a handy spot,' he said, handing out lumps of bread from his saddlebag and passing round a leather flask of wine.

He told them his name was Oreb.

'*Sir* Oreb?' Hagab asked.

Oreb laughed.

'I don't think so, friend,' he said. 'The people round here have rather less complimentary titles for me than that!'

The friends were all completely confused about what was going on. Thassi knew it was time he took some kind of lead.

'What *are* you then, if you're not a knight?' he asked. 'Are we your prisoners?'

'If people want to be polite, they call me a reaver,' Oreb told them. 'If they don't, they call me a thief – or worse. I like to think of myself as a kind of taxman.' From the little rocky hilltop, they could see quite a long way and Oreb stretched his arms out, pointing east and west.

'All this is my patch,' he said. 'Anyone I catch crossing the border from the Old Kingdom to the Northern Realm, or the other way round, risks a challenge. If I beat them, they give me their money, if not... well, that doesn't really happen very often. I'm quite choosy about who I challenge!' He laughed, and they found that they were laughing with him. 'Oh – and if they don't *have* any money—' he paused and grinned at them '—they get a free lunch and go on their way! But *that* doesn't happen very often either!'

'And who do you collect the taxes *for*?' Jaala asked.

Oreb looked at him as if he was mad. 'Oh, come *on*, friend – use your brains!' he said and patted the fat leather pouch hanging at his belt.

He explained that there were reavers operating all along the border. They tried not to get in each other's way. If times were hard, they might even band together to raid one of the local villages – north or south of the border. They weren't fussy. They made a pretty good living out of their activities and most of them lived in fortified towers dotted along the borderlands. Oreb's was half a day's ride to the east.

'I'd invite you to stay, friends,' he said. 'I've taken rather a liking to you. But I'm not going to be home for a while. It's going to be free passage across this stretch of the border for the rest of the year. You might well be my last customers until I get back. I'm heading south – to Earl Melech's castle. I don't suppose any of you knows the way, do you?'

'We don't,' said Shual, 'but we wish we were going with you.'

'Oho! So you'd like to join the Tournament too, would you? And what would you fight with? Your bare hands?'

He laughed and the friends looked embarrassed. Inside, all of them were seething, even Thassi. They hadn't been able to believe it when Baladan had said they had to leave their weapons back at Rakath's castle. They'd sweated and bargained for those weapons.

'Still, I don't blame you for wanting to go,' Oreb went on. 'There's good money to be won, so everyone says. I might even be able to retire on it if I win.'

'You'll only do that if you fight for Abaddon,' Saraf told him. 'Everywhere we've been, people are tipping him for Champion.'

'Hard man, is he?' Oreb asked.

'He's sent messengers round the Kingdom threatening to carve up anyone who doesn't support him,' Thassi explained. 'Everywhere we've been, we've heard of knights joining him because they're frightened they'll find their castles burned out if they don't.'

'Plenty of others he's just bribed,' Saraf put in.

'Now you're talking,' Oreb said. 'Threats don't interest me much but bribery's another matter. I might consider joining him at that, if the price is right. Who is this Abaddon, anyway?'

'You should get on like a house on fire,' said Shual. 'He's a robber.'

Oreb stared hard at Shual, and for the first time the friends saw something steely in the reaver's eyes.

'Manners, friend,' he said, his voice very low and cold. 'Don't push your luck.'

No one wanted to be the first to speak after that, and Oreb let the silence last for some time before he broke it himself.

'So, tell me,' he said at last, 'apart from having nothing to fight with, what else is keeping you from the Tournament? Have you some business in these parts? I hope you weren't planning to buy anything, because I have to tell you, friends, they expect people to *pay* for things over the border.'

Thassi told him about Baladan's orders and Saraf, backed by all the rest, went through the arguments for giving up their journey.

'Well, friends,' Oreb said, 'if you want my advice, I think you've done all that this Baladan could ask of you. If I were you, I'd be heading south again.'

'But we don't know if he *wants* us to go south,' Thassi insisted. 'We don't know *where* we're supposed to go until we get a message.'

Oreb put his arm round Thassi's shoulder.

'Listen, friend,' he said, 'it is *not* going to be north, that's for sure. Up there, you'll find nothing but animals dressed in trousers. If it makes you feel any better, why don't we say *I'm* bringing you a message from this Baladan? He says, "Head on south, boys. Meet me at Melech's castle".'

'But that's *not* a message from Baladan,' Thassi said, shrugging off Oreb's arm.

'How do *you* know?' the reaver asked. 'Are you calling me a liar?'

So Thassi and his friends found themselves travelling south, with Oreb as their guide and guardian.

'If you can't give me any money, friends – at least you can give me your company,' he'd said.

Then he'd drawn a knife quicker than you could blink and had held it at Jaala's throat.

'Or perhaps I'll just sell you as slaves,' he'd added, going into a fit of laughter that, for once, no one else shared.

On their second day together, they were tramping along a rough track at the bottom of a deep ravine. Spring seemed to be struggling to show itself this far north and there were still pockets of snow high up on the hills which penned them in on either side.

But it wasn't the snow which caught Thassi's attention. Something had moved up there, way up on the right. He was certain he'd seen something – a tiny scrap of colour – disappearing behind one of the twisted bushes clinging to the sides of the ravine. And Thassi remembered that a couple of times earlier that day, he'd heard the clatter of falling rocks above them. He was sure they were being followed. He slowed up to let Oreb catch him. The reaver had stayed mounted but he was walking his pony slowly behind them all, guarding their rear.

'We're being followed,' Thassi whispered, without looking up at Oreb.

'I know,' Oreb replied, looking straight ahead. 'High, right. He was there yesterday, too. And he paid us a visit last night.'

'What?'

'Took some food from one of my saddlebags. Either that or the animals round here can undo buckles.'

They walked on in silence for a few moments.

'We'll never catch him on those slopes,' Thassi said at last.

'So?'

'If he's risking stealing food, he must be hungry.'

Oreb nodded.

'So he'll be back tonight,' Thassi went on. 'We'll wait up for him.'

'I'm glad you said that,' Oreb told him.

'Why?'

'Because now *you* can do it, friend. I thought *I* was going to have to lose a night's sleep to trap him.'

<hr />

There was no cloud cover that night, which meant it was freezing. But Thassi was glad. It also meant there was nothing covering the full moon, so he had a good view of the saddlebags Oreb had left out in the middle of their camp. They'd bedded down ages ago and Thassi could hear snoring and snuffling all around him. He was beginning to wonder if the brightness of the moon had put the raider off, but then he saw a movement beside a barricade of bushes where the steep hillside met the valley bottom. Thassi's muscles were stiff with the cold and he started to flex them under the thick woollen cloak which served as a blanket. His hand was on the handle of the knife Oreb had lent him. He didn't have much longer to wait. A moment later, he saw a figure dart from the bushes to a nearby rock. Big rocks littered the ground almost up to their camp and the figure came towards him in silent zigzag bursts from rock to rock. At last there was no cover left, and the raider crept forward in the full light of the moon, slow and careful as a stalking cat. It was then that Thassi realised the intruder was a boy, maybe no older than Ruel.

That wasn't the only surprising thing about him. He looked nothing like any of the people Thassi had ever seen anywhere in the Old Kingdom. And he looked rich. A heavy metal torc glinted round his neck and his long red hair was held back by a fancy headband. A flashy-looking brooch pinned his cloak together on his shoulder and his bare arms were covered in swirly, spiral tattoos and fine metal rings. Thassi got a good look at all this detail as the boy inched his way towards the saddlebags. The instant he reached them, Thassi pounced.

Then everything seemed to explode. The boy somehow twisted on his back and came up spitting and scratching like a wild animal. He might have been young but he clearly wasn't going to be a pushover. Seeing the raider's age, Thassi had left Oreb's knife behind. Now he wished he hadn't. He struggled for a few seconds, trying to pin down the boy's thrashing arms, then a knee smacked up hard between his legs and he rolled away in agony. Through the stars and coloured lights flashing in front of his eyes, he saw another body throwing itself at the intruder. Oreb. There was a lot of grunting, shouting and swearing as the rest of the party joined in, then everything went quiet. It had taken three of them to pin the boy down and in the end Oreb had to hold his sword to his throat to force him to lie still. When Thassi staggered to his feet, it looked as if there'd been a full-scale battle in the camp.

'A fine specimen,' Oreb said. 'Maybe I won't need to go to the Tournament after all to pay for my retirement. I knew you lot would bring me luck.'

'What are you talking about?' Thassi asked, rubbing himself and trying to stand up straight.

'All this fancy stuff should bring in some cash,' Oreb said, bending and pulling the torc off the boy's neck as Shual and Saraf held him down.

The boy writhed and let out a burst of rough, throaty words that sounded as if he was going to spit. The friends couldn't understand a bit of it, but to their surprise, Oreb fired off back at him in the same language. They went on for quite a while till it seemed that Oreb had heard enough.

'Tie him up,' he ordered.

'Just a minute,' Thassi protested. 'Who is he? What's going on?'

Oreb heaved a sigh.

'He's a chieftain's son, from the Northern Realm. That's why he's loaded with jewellery. And he'll fetch a good ransom, I can tell you. So can we get on with the business now? There's some rope in my—'

'But what's he *doing* here?' Thassi butted in. 'Why was he following us?'

'Listen, friend, have you ever heard the phrase "don't look a gift horse in the mouth"?' Oreb asked.

There was an edge to his voice, and he was obviously losing his temper. He turned back to the boy, still pinned to the ground by Shual and Saraf, and questioned him some more in the strange northern language.

'Says they've a dragon in their land,' Oreb reported. 'Reckons they've heard there's a dragon slayer operating in the Old Kingdom. He says he decided to run away from home and persuade this dragon slayer to come and save his father's lands. When he saw me riding along with you, he had some strange idea that maybe *I* was his man. He was trailing us to check us out. Oh, and he'd also run out of food – thieving animal.'

Oreb looked down at the wriggling boy with complete contempt and pressed his sword point back into the lad's throat until he lay still again.

'Bad mistake, lion cub – bad mistake,' he said, in the language of the Old Kingdom. 'Think yourself lucky you're worth more alive than dead. Your daddy must be going mad just now.' Oreb turned back to Thassi. 'Now are *you* going to tie him up, or am I? But I'll tell you, if I have to do it, you don't get a thing out of this deal.'

This was the last straw for Thassi. Oreb might be armed and dangerous, but there were still five of them, and the boy would probably join in on their side once he worked out what was going on. He squared up to the reaver.

'We don't *want* anything from your deal,' he said, steadily. 'We don't want anything to do with this. It's not you the boy was looking for – it's us. *Baladan's* the dragon slayer, and he's sent *us* to take care of things like this.' He turned to his four friends. 'Don't you *see?*' he said. 'This is it – this must be the reason we've come all this way!'

There was silence then Saraf and Shual pulled the boy onto his feet, twisting his arms behind him.

'Where's the rope?' Saraf asked.

'Good man,' Oreb said, sheathing his sword. 'That bag on the right.'

Jaala went to get it.

'What are you doing?' Thassi shouted.

'What are *you* doing?' Hagab fired off, going to help Jaala unravel the rope. 'The Northern Realm has nothing to do with us. If we're going to do some fighting, the Tournament's the place to do it.'

'*With* some proper weapons,' Shual put in. 'And if we get a cut out of this deal, we'll be able to buy some.'

'Well spoken, friends,' Oreb said, his voice calm and friendly again. 'The best thing you can do for these northern animals is to let the dragon eat them all. That's my advice.'

'No!' Thassi shouted. He dived for the cloak he'd been using as bedding and came up holding Oreb's knife. He stood facing them all, scanning his friends' faces for support.

'This isn't what Baladan wants,' he said.

Everything froze for a moment then Oreb gave a hard little laugh. 'How do *you* know, my friend?' he asked.

'He knows well enough,' said a familiar voice from the bushes where the boy had been hiding.

They all swung round and saw a thin-faced figure, in old leather clothes, standing tall in the moonlight. It was easy to forget how tall Baladan was, but he stood a head higher than Oreb. The reaver stepped out towards him, sword at the ready.

'I thought you were "quite choosy" about the people you challenged,' said Baladan.

His battle sword hung down his back, the hilt visible over his left shoulder. He reached his right hand casually across his chest and rested it lightly on the massive hilt. There was a moment's pause.

The camp seemed to shimmer in a strange light. It looked like silver moonlight but seemed to be coming in ripples from the sphere on the hilt of Baladan's sword. Oreb took a step back and sheathed his weapon, making a gesture of welcome.

'Good choice – "friend",' Baladan told him. Then he turned to Thassi and smiled.

'Set the boy free,' he said, 'and give him something to eat – he's hungry.'

Baladan helped make a fire. They all gathered round it, and as the boy ate, Baladan talked to him. Thassi and his friends realised it wasn't surprising that a border reaver could speak the language of the Northern Realm, but here was Baladan, too, talking easily to the boy in his own language. More amazing than that, now that the words were being spoken more gently and slowly, they realised they could recognise some of them themselves. As they tuned in and concentrated, they could even understand the gist of the conversation.

When the chieftain's son had eaten, Baladan started negotiations with him. After a little persuasion, the lad stood up in the middle of them all and cleared his throat.

'Did you understand what I asked him to do?' Baladan whispered to Thassi.

'You asked him about the kings of the Northern Realm,' Thassi said. 'Something about reciting the poem of their kings.'

'That's it,' said Baladan. 'He's going to do it. He's a bright lad – nephew of a king himself. Listen.'

The boy made a start, hesitating at first but getting into full flow as he picked up confidence. Oreb sloped off in disgust and bedded down again out of the firelight, but the others, keen to be back in Baladan's good books, sat tight and tried to understand what the boy was saying. Strangely enough, now it was turned into poetry, the northern language didn't sound so ugly. It sounded rather grand, in fact, and the friends could understand quite a bit of it.

Every land had its 'poem of the kings' – the story of all those who had ruled the land and their exploits from the beginning of time. It was the kind of thing someone would recite in the evening for after-dinner entertainment. The Old Kingdom had such a poem. Zilla knew it and had taught it to Ruel. He'd often recited it in the castle hall at Kiriath.

However, there was a problem with the Old Kingdom's poem: it ran out of kings at a time way before even Zilla had been born. Zilla had once told Ruel that was why people called it the 'Old' Kingdom – because it didn't have a king any more. Not that Zilla and Ruel believed that. They were both sure there *was* a king somewhere, if only he could be found. When he'd lost his sister, Ruel had set out to search for the King to help rescue her. He'd never found him but he had found Baladan instead.

As the boy's poem wound on, a strange thing started to

happen. Thassi and his friends began to recognise some of the names in it: at first just a few they knew from their own poem because they were people who'd done battle with the Old Kingdom. But then, as the poem went further back in time, they recognised three names in a row, then four, then five – and these weren't people who'd *fought* Old Kingdom kings. They *were* Old Kingdom kings!

The boy finished his poem and Baladan and his friends gave him a round of applause. The lad tried to look stern and dignified as he bowed, but they caught sight of a little smile at the corners of his mouth.

'Notice anything?' Baladan asked Thassi, beckoning the boy to sit with them.

'The kings were the same,' Thassi told him. 'At the end, they were all the same as our kings! And the things they did – all the same as in *our* poem.'

'And what do you learn from that?'

Thassi was puzzled and silent. It was Shual who came up with the answer.

'Does it mean the Northern Realm and the Old Kingdom started off as the same land?' he asked.

'Exactly,' Baladan told him. 'Same kings, same language, same people. Go back far enough and you'll find there *aren't* any foreigners any more. So maybe this northern dragon *is* your business after all. Think about it. Sleep on it.'

In the morning, when the friends stretched their stiff limbs and shook out their cloaks, they found that Oreb had gone.

'He was up before dawn,' Baladan told them. 'I said he could come north and win a share of the dragon's hoard but he reckoned he'd never heard of anyone getting their hands on a dragon's treasure before – not even an oversized peasant with a big sword, like me! Nice turn of phrase! He seemed to think the prize money at the Tournament was a better risk. He can't be too far ahead, though – join him if you want to.'

There was a pause. The four friends looked at each other, then at Thassi. Thassi took a step forward to stand by Baladan and the boy. A moment later, the others followed.

'Good,' said Baladan. 'This won't take long. Other people's dragons are always much less trouble than your own.'

CHAPTER FOUR

hassi's friends were right. Lexa and Rizpa *were* having an easy time on the journey Baladan had given them. And Lexa was ready to admit it when Zethar ran into her one day in early May. Zethar had been walking since dawn and when he saw a scatter of ruins in the distance, he made for them to take a breather. He found Lexa sitting against a crumbling perimeter wall and joined her to rest on the rich green grass. The wall had been soaking up the sun all morning and warmed their backs as they talked, so they should have been relaxed, but they were both edgy.

'Rizpa and I ought to be enjoying ourselves,' Lexa said. '"Make for the south coast and head east along it." Those were our orders and what better place could we be? Soft, rolling downs – green, peaceful and much hotter than it would be back home in Maon this time of year. Friendly people and not even the rumour of a monster.'

'So what's the problem?' Zethar asked.

Lexa paused for a moment but knew she had to say what was weighing on her mind.

'It's Rizpa,' she said. '*She's* been the monster on this trip.'

Zethar looked round. 'Where *is* Rizpa?' he asked.

'You tell me!' Lexa said. 'Somewhere around here.' And she waved impatiently at the stretch of ruins in front of them. 'She's gone exploring.'

The place had obviously been a castle long ago, and a very big one, too. The outer wall against which Lexa and Zethar were leaning surrounded an area the size of several fields. About two hundred metres in front of them were the remains of an inner wall surrounding a cylindrical tower – the hub of the whole complex. The space between outer and inner walls was littered with the remains of buildings.

'I don't understand it,' Lexa told Zethar. 'Rizpa and I have always been close – and how could anything come between us after what happened with The Dragon last year?'

The previous year, Lexa's home village of Maon, just north of Hazar, had sent her as their sacrifice to the Kiriath Dragon but Rizpa had refused to be parted from her sister so the two had gone to their doom together. It was only the appearance of Baladan that had saved them.

'It's been tough in Maon,' Lexa explained, 'since nearly all the men died fighting The Dragon three years ago. I suppose this is the first opportunity Rizpa and I have had to spend time alone together with no pressures. It should be good – but somehow there seems to be this tension all the time. I feel as if something in the air needs clearing and I don't know what it is.'

In normal circumstances, Zethar wasn't the person Lexa would have chosen to share her feelings. He usually frightened her – there was something wild, unsettling, unpredictable about him. But she'd been desperate to talk for days and there was no one else. Her need to talk was so strong that it prevented her taking much notice of Zethar's mood until she'd finished speaking. Then she began to sense that he, too, was on edge. Insects buzzed, the sun warmed them and it was very soothing, but Zethar was sitting forward with his arms tight round his knees, chewing savagely on a grass stalk. He was staring into the distance and there seemed to be some new quality in him, some uncertainty, that she hadn't seen before.

'How are *you*?' she said. 'Where are you going?'

'Anywhere,' he said. 'Everywhere.'

There was a pause and he chewed more fiercely.

'What are you supposed to be doing?' she asked.

'I have to find something,' he told her.

She waited but he didn't say more.

'What is it?' she asked.

Zethar was still staring across the ruins and she realised he hadn't looked at her since their first greeting. 'I can't say,' he told her.

Just then a head, surrounded by masses of copper hair, popped up over the wall of a collapsed building about a hundred metres in front of them.

'*There* she is!' Lexa said. She didn't exactly look pleased to see her sister.

The head disappeared again.

'I *warned* her about climbing about inside those buildings. The walls could fall and crush her. She's such a *child* sometimes! Wait here,' she told Zethar and set off to fetch Rizpa.

When she'd persuaded her sister to come out of the ruined building, Lexa pointed to the place she'd left Zethar. But he wasn't there. A moment later, they picked out his figure tramping away across the downs. He looked slightly stooped – burdened. Rizpa shouted after him at the top of her loud voice, but he didn't turn round.

'Charming!' she said, then shrugged her shoulders and turned her attention back to exploration.

Despite her sister's protests, Rizpa clambered up the outside of the building and stood on the top of its crumbled wall, looking round the site intently.

'There's something odd about this place,' she said after a minute.

'Yes, it's all fallen down,' Lexa said, impatiently.

'No, apart from that. It feels sort of "looked after". None of this old stonework is overgrown, is it? And the grass is short – why's that?'

'Something to do with those?' Lexa suggested sarcastically, pointing to several white blobs on the far side of the castle's outer area.

'Yes, but who do the sheep *belong* to?' Rizpa asked. 'And what about the flowers all over the place? Everywhere there's some old stonework, it's surrounded by a bed of flowers. They don't look as if they've just *grown* there. They look as if they've been planted to make the place look nice. And I'll tell you something else, that tower right in the middle of everything doesn't seem damaged at all. It looks as if someone might still live in it. Let's go and see.'

And without waiting for a reply, she went.

***

When the sisters had gone through the gateway in the inner wall, they saw the central tower was ringed by a moat. There'd been a dry ditch around the first outer wall but this moat was full of water. It was clean, too – not the rank, stagnant water you'd expect from somewhere which had been abandoned for years.

'Oh, look!' said Rizpa, suddenly. 'Look at those! They're beautiful!'

A pair of dazzling white swans had just come paddling round the moat from behind the tower.

'And what on earth are *they*?'

Rizpa was pointing at some fat fish, swimming lazily. There were lots of them and their brilliant orange colour shone through the clear water. Just then, music started trickling gently through the air. It sounded like the minstrels' harps they'd heard at Kiriath and at Rakath's castle, and seemed to prove there really *must* be someone in the tower. The music was so beautiful and the scene and the sounds seemed to be in such perfect harmony that even Lexa had no words of caution to say. The sisters simply listened, looked and enjoyed until the music stopped. Then they walked slowly round the tower and on the far side, they found a lowered drawbridge. They crossed it and Rizpa blew the horn hanging by the studded wooden door. Again, there was no sign of decay – the timber was solid and the horn clean and polished.

The man who eventually opened the door had the same effect on Rizpa as the swans, although she managed not to comment out loud. He must have been in his mid-twenties and had shoulder-length hair which matched the colour of his fish. He had blue eyes and these, with his orange hair, made him a dazzling sight in the bright sunlight. Rizpa wanted to keep on looking, but found herself lowering her eyes instead.

'Ladies! Come in!' he said, and his voice was as light and tuneful as the harp.

He wore a deep green velvet cloak which swished as he turned round to lead them in. He took them into a circular room which took up the whole of the ground floor of the tower.

'Welcome to my hall,' he said, almost singing the words.

On a platform at the far side of the room stood a high table. On a green velvet cushion in the middle of the table was a golden bell. The man went over and rang the bell. Like everything else, it sounded beautiful.

The torches bracketed to the walls were unlit, so the only light came through the narrow windows, but the sisters could see that the place was decorated with hanging tapestries. They glowed with gold thread, and dragons were being gracefully executed in every one.

'Ah, my tapestries!' the man said, seeing them looking round. 'The records of noble deeds. Tales of dragon slaying are the delight of my life.'

A servant entered and placed a tray of drinks on the table.

'That and the company of beautiful young ladies,' the man said, handing a silver goblet of wine to Rizpa.

He smiled at her and bowed. She blushed – not something she did often.

'I think we ought to tell you we're not "ladies",' Lexa told him quietly as he gave her a goblet. 'We're just villagers on a long journey.'

'To me,' he said, with a grand sweep of his arm, 'every beautiful woman is a lady – their very beauty makes them noble. Come and join me.' And he motioned for them to sit with him at the high table.

He introduced himself as Lord Zemira, the owner of the castle. It was the biggest in the whole of the land, he told them proudly – or it had been in its heyday. Now he was the only person who lived there, apart from his servants.

'But soon, I hope to return both this noble place and my family name to their former glory,' he told them. 'I, too, am going on a long journey – far away to the castle of Earl Melech.'

'To the Tournament?' Rizpa asked.

'Yes, indeed, my lady,' he replied. 'With every hope of winning, and going on to destroy the power of the dragons for ever.'

He clapped his hands, as if the task would be as easy as smacking a fly, and leaned back in his seat, well satisfied. The ancient carved wooden seat looked as if it was made for a much bigger man. Rizpa realised that although Lord Zemira was tall, he was quite thin and frail-looking. He had long thin fingers and his skin was very white.

'Really?' said Lexa. 'We've been hearing that Abaddon's the favourite to win.'

Lord Zemira threw back his head and gave a harsh little laugh.

'Abaddon?' he said. 'He's nothing but a peasant! A robber and a scoundrel! How could he stand up against a true gentleman – a man of noble blood?' He held out his delicate white hands and looked at them. 'Blood of the highest quality runs in these veins,' he said, in a low, reverent voice. 'They say it was once the royal blood,' he added in a whisper.

His face had turned serious to match his voice and he leaned forward towards Rizpa.

'Lady—' he said.

'You shouldn't keep calling her that,' Lexa told him, but he ignored her.

'Lady, out of your kindness and charity, would you allow me to wear your favour at the Tournament?'

'Do what?' Rizpa asked.

'To wear your scarf or girdle wound about my helmet – to show that I fight in your name, and that all the glory I win is dedicated to you.'

'She doesn't *have* a scarf or a girdle,' Lexa put in.

'No matter,' said Lord Zemira, clapping his hands again. 'Come and see my armour.'

'And you don't *know* her name,' Lexa muttered to herself, as they rose from the table.

He led them up a staircase built into the thickness of the tower wall, and on the next floor, they found themselves in another circular room where every inch of the curved wall was hung with swords, pikes, axes, shields, helmets and body armour.

'All that's left to me from the generations who went before,' he said.

In the middle of the room, a full suit of armour had been made up and stood there like a guard. It had been put in the spot where it caught maximum light from all the window slits.

'See,' said Lord Zemira, pointing to the helmet. A bright red scarf was already wound around it. 'We'll call it yours,' he said.

'But it's not,' Lexa pointed out.

'Oh, shut up!' Rizpa whispered.

Rizpa was as aware as Lexa of the tension that had been growing between them and it upset and puzzled her, too. An argument had been brewing all morning, looking for an excuse to break out. Rizpa had gone exploring earlier to try to avoid an explosion.

Lord Zemira clearly wanted to show them the whole tower so on they went, up another staircase.

'Maybe he doesn't get many visitors,' Rizpa whispered to her sister as they followed the swishing green robe.

'I wonder why!' Lexa replied.

Rizpa wanted to turn on her sister and tell her to stop taking her bad temper out on their host, but she let it go.

The cylindrical wall of the next room had huge curved cupboards cut into it, full of books. On a big round wooden table in the middle of the room lay several open volumes and half a dozen snuffed out candles. The place smelled of beeswax and old leather.

'My library,' Lord Zemira announced, pointing to one of the cupboards. 'Poetry and music – all the songs of the greatest heroes in the world.' Then he moved close to Rizpa. 'And the greatest lovers,' he added, softly.

'Oh, for heaven's sake,' Lexa muttered. She went to look out of one of the windows.

'Here,' he said, taking Rizpa's hand and leading her to the table. 'These are rare books on chivalry – the art of knighthood. I have two cupboards full of them. Look, here it tells you about the wearing of a lady's favour—'

'She can't read,' Lexa said, from the window.

'Will you *shut up!*' Rizpa hissed.

'And now, ladies,' said Lord Zemira, letting go of Rizpa and going to a curtained doorway that led to the next staircase, 'will you honour me by visiting my chamber?'

'Absolutely not!' Lexa blazed. 'Come on, Rizpa, we're leaving!'

'What's the *matter* with you?' Rizpa snapped.

'Can't you see what he's after?' her sister replied.

'Oh, come on,' Rizpa said. 'He's not made of much. We could flatten him if he tries anything on.'

'How do you know there aren't half a dozen of his servants up there?' Lexa pointed out.

'Ladies!' Lord Zemira protested. 'I have spent my life devoted to chivalry – no man who follows the code of knighthood would harm a lady. My chamber is where I keep my harp. It's where I play and sing. All I wanted was to *sing* to you.'

'You can do that here,' said Lexa, unmoved.

'But there aren't any seats for you.'

'We'll stand,' Lexa replied.

There was obviously no arguing with Lexa, so Lord Zemira went to fetch his instrument. Rizpa was amazed at her sister challenging a lord, even such a wishy-washy one. And Lexa wasn't finished yet.

'Wait here,' she told Rizpa. 'And if he tries anything while I'm away, run for it.'

With that she was off down the stairs to the floor below. By the time Zemira returned, Lexa was standing beside her sister again. The only difference was that now they both held swords from the armoury.

'Ladies!' said Lord Zemira, in a voice almost choked with shock.

'*We're* quite keen on the art of knighthood, too,' said Lexa. 'We can use these, so be warned.'

Lord Zemira was speechless. But he wasn't going to let

the sight of 'ladies' with swords spoil his performance, so he settled himself in the chair at the big desk and tried a few runs on his harp. Soon the argument seemed to pass out of his mind. He no longer appeared to know there was anyone else in the room. He closed his eyes, cocked his head on one side and started to sing.

Lexa hadn't really been worried that Zemira would molest them, but something in the whole situation was stirring her up unbearably. But as Zemira played and sang, she found that, despite herself, she started to relax. They'd already heard his harp playing from outside the castle, but Zemira's singing voice was just as good and the two together were breathtaking. The song was beautiful – not just the tune, but the words, too. It was about a young man who'd lost his love, and the way he sang, it sounded as if it was about Lord Zemira himself.

The sisters had propped their swords against the wall. When the song was over, Rizpa clapped loudly and Lexa dabbed her eyes quickly on her sleeve.

'When did you lose her?' she asked, quietly.

'Lose who?' asked Zemira, puzzled.

'The woman in the song.'

'Oh, she's not *real*,' he said, with a laugh. 'Good heavens, no. I made it up! I make one up nearly every day. I have hundreds – shall I sing you another?'

Lexa stared at him with an odd, crumpled look.

'Aren't *any* of them true?' she asked.

'Well, it depends what you mean by "true", my lady – true to life, I hope, true in their feelings, but not in the characters – this is Art, after all!'

'So haven't you *ever* lost someone you love?' she asked.

'I'm most thankful to say I haven't,' the young Lord replied, with a charming smile.

'You've no right,' said Lexa, quietly. 'You've no right

to steal feelings you haven't had. It's as if you're making fun of them.'

Rizpa had had enough. 'Lexa!' she said. 'You've done nothing but criticise Lord Zemira since we got here. You're just cross because he's paying me attention, that's all.'

'Don't be ridiculous,' her sister replied.

There was a moment's pause as they eyed each other dangerously.

'Just because you've got a problem about men—' Rizpa muttered.

'I have *not*!' Lexa snapped.

There was another pause. Rizpa knew it was her last chance to drop the subject, but she didn't take it.

'What about Thassi, then?' she said. 'He seems keen enough on you, but every time he tries to be nice, you just ignore him.'

'Maybe I don't like him,' Lexa replied.

'He's not the first, either,' Rizpa went on. 'Chilion tried before that. Just because none of them measures up to your precious Tola! You can't spend your life looking for another just like him.'

Lexa put her hands over her face.

Rizpa knew what pictures her sister would be seeing behind those hands. She saw them herself often enough, even with her eyes open, pictures which would never go away for either of them. Maon village, three years ago – brave men marching out to fight The Dragon – hours later, nothing but broken weapons and charred remains. Women weeping everywhere. Rizpa was aware she'd stepped into forbidden territory but felt there was no going back now. She pressed on, almost with a sense of relief.

'It's not your own private tragedy,' she said. 'Tola wasn't the only person killed fighting The Dragon that day. Get over it. Everyone else had to. I don't know why it was such a big deal, anyway. You'd only been together a few months! You couldn't have *loved* him!'

Lexa's hands dropped from her face.

'What do you know about it?' she said. 'You don't know anything *about* love!'

For a moment, it looked as if the pair of them might start a fight and Lord Zemira stepped between them, his arms spread wide.

'Ladies, ladies!' he pleaded.

Rizpa pushed him out of the way.

'Just you listen!' she told her sister. 'I'll tell you about love. I might never have had a boyfriend like you, but my *father* died fighting that dragon. My *father* – have you got that? My own flesh and blood – the best man in the world. And he was *your* father, too, although you'd never have known it at the time. Did you give one *minute's* thought to me and Mum while you were busy weeping and wailing over Tola? *Did* you?'

'Why *shouldn't* I weep over him?' Lexa shouted. 'We were going to get *married*! But who wanted to know about that? Who wanted to weep with a "widow" who'd never been married when there was a village full of *real* widows to weep with? Not *you*. You never even *considered* me. Not one kind word did I get from you, not *one!*'

The sisters stared at each other, breathing hard. In the silence, the three of them suddenly realised the room was darkening. Something outside was closing in on them. Almost as soon as they realised what was happening, the darkness came right up to the windows and completely sealed them off. Everything went absolutely black. There was a moment's stunned silence then Lord Zemira let out a most unmusical sound.

'Torches,' he yelled. 'Bring torches!'

Five minutes later, servants had fixed torches in the brackets around the room, lit the candles on the reading desk and ventured out onto the tower roof to see what had happened. They reported that a giant serpent had coiled itself round the tower from top to bottom, covering the door and every window. In the torchlight, Lord Zemira and the sisters could see its scales shining like green plates of armour across each unglazed window. Rizpa went over to one and touched the skin of the serpent. It felt smooth and strong as steel, but warm, as if there was fire inside. She pulled her hand back in surprise.

'We have to do something,' said Lexa, turning to Lord Zemira. 'There must be some way of moving it. What do you know about it? Has it attacked you before?'

Zemira was sitting at his desk, holding his harp to his chest.

'There haven't been any monsters in this land for years,' he said. 'Everything was peaceful – until you turned up.'

'Useless,' Rizpa muttered.

She picked up a sword and bracing it across her chest, she ran at one of the windows and stabbed the scales with all her force. The sword just twisted out of her grip and clattered to the stone floor. Rizpa rubbed her wrists and examined the scales. There wasn't a scratch on them.

Lexa took a torch from one of the wall brackets and carried it towards a window.

'Good idea,' said Rizpa. 'Come on!' and she held out a torch to Zemira.

Obediently, he took it and they all positioned themselves at separate windows.

'Now!' said Lexa, and they each held their torches

against the scaly skin.

Seconds passed. Nothing happened, except that they seemed to be shaking. Then there was a thud. They looked round and saw that a book had fallen out of one of the cupboards. Another thud, then another. As they watched, more books began to jiggle towards the edge of their shelves. Then they realised it was the *tower* that was shaking. They could feel it under their feet now. Large chunks of plaster started falling off the walls around them. The serpent was squeezing the tower.

'Stop!' said Lexa.

They moved their torches away from the serpent's skin to see what damage they'd done. Nothing. The scales were as shiny and strong as before.

The serpent kept on tightening its grip. Soon every book had been shaken off its shelf onto the floor. Zemira was under the table, protecting some of his most treasured volumes and his harp. The servants had fled to the cellars, the sisters were up to their ankles in fallen plaster and the room was full of dust. Now they could hear a grating and groaning as the stones of the tower started to shift under the pressure. It was only a matter of time before the tower ended up as a heap of rubble like the rest of the castle. They would be crushed to pulp inside it.

The only alternative would be to head for the cellars with the servants, but with a collapsed tower on top of them, they'd never get out. They both knew they were going to die. It was just a question of whether it would be slowly in the cellars or quickly where they stood.

Rizpa took her sister's hands. 'Shall we stay here?' she said.

Lexa nodded and the two of them moved closer, clinging on to each other tightly.

'I'm sorry,' Lexa whispered.

'Me, too,' her sister said.

They both had their eyes closed, tears wetting their cheeks. Suddenly Rizpa felt someone wiping her face. For an instant she thought it must be Lexa but then she realised her sister still had both arms round her. She opened her eyes in surprise and saw Baladan, now wiping Lexa's tears. The room seemed brighter, but she realised the windows were still tightly sealed. The light was coming from inside. Then Lexa saw it was glowing from Baladan's sword. The sword was hanging behind his back, the handle showing over his shoulder, with the orb at the end shining like a little sun. At first, Lexa thought it was reflecting light from the torches then she realised that the light from the orb was brighter than anything else. She also noticed that the room had stopped shaking.

'We tried a sword on the serpent,' Rizpa said, 'but it didn't even scratch the scales.'

Baladan looked at the weapons, half-buried among the fragments of plaster.

'This needs something more powerful than a sword,' he said and he walked to a window with the cloth he had used to wipe their tears. He held it against the serpent's skin and immediately the scales started to bubble. The room was filled with an awful smell like rotten eggs and there was a terrible, tearing scream outside. Daylight began to seep in at the windows. Soon it was streaming in, and the sisters rushed to look out. The serpent had slipped down the tower and lay in a wrinkled heap, like a fallen stocking. It was shrivelling and shrinking, and a moment later, it fell right into the moat, thrashing in agony. Soon it was no bigger than an eel. The swans had flown when the serpent appeared but now one of them returned, glided up to the shrivelling creature, snapped its back with its beak and threw it away. It sank slowly and the fish nibbled it to nothing.

Rizpa and Lexa turned back to the room to ask Baladan how he'd got into the tower. But he was gone.

'Zemira – did you see someone else in the room?' Rizpa asked. 'A tall man, long dark hair, old leather clothes, eyes that—'

'There's no point in asking him,' Lexa butted in.

It was true. Lord Zemira was still under the table, his hands over his eyes.

'You can come out now, my lord,' Rizpa told him. 'It's over.'

As Rizpa and Lexa walked towards the remains of the outer castle wall in the light of the sinking sun, they heard the distant sound of a harp, then the voice of Lord Zemira came drifting through the air from his tower. They thought they caught some words about a serpent, a daring young lord and the fearless strokes of his mighty sword. Then the sisters set off on the road Zethar had taken earlier and Zemira's music faded behind them, lost in the twittering of the early evening birds.

chapter five

abad was sitting on an ancient stone bench by a pool, staring into its green depths. The water was clear: the green colour came from the mosses around it and the weeds below its surface. It seemed it was also reflecting green from their surroundings – a long, deep valley of lush, peaceful greenery, mostly ferns and shrubs. They were a long way from the nearest village. The only sound was running water, so tranquil that Zabad seemed to have gone into a trance. It was half an hour since he'd told Zilla he needed a rest and she was ready to travel on now, but he didn't look as if he meant to move for the rest of the day.

'I'd like to stay here,' he said at last, in a distant sort of voice.

'We can camp overnight, if you're really so tired, dearie,' Zilla told him.

'I meant for ever,' said Zabad.

The pool was made by a nearby spring which gurgled from the base of a rocky outcrop in the valley side. In the rock was a cave which had obviously been lived in long ago. Its mouth had been walled in to make a proper doorway, though the door had long since rotted to nothing. Inside, the rock had been shaped to make ledges for sleeping and storage. They'd explored it before sitting down to rest.

'I wonder who used to live here,' Zabad went on. 'We're miles from anywhere. It must have been some kind of hermit – someone who wanted to get away from it all.'

'Or *run* away from it all,' Zilla suggested. 'Come on. You *can't* stay here for ever. We have a job to do. Baladan told us to keep heading east till we got word to join him.'

Zabad glanced up into her face. He looked suddenly desperate.

'I'm old,' he said.

'Nonsense,' Zilla told him. 'You're only in your fifties. *I'm* old – I was already a young woman when you were born. If you don't want to camp, let's move – we can walk for another couple of hours before nightfall.'

But Zabad didn't stir. He poked at the pool with a stick, sending ripples across it, then watched it settle again.

'I can't,' he said at last.

'Can't *what*?'

'Go on – not *that* way, anyway.' Without looking up, Zabad pointed east down the valley. 'Can't we go north or south for a while then pick up going east again?'

Zilla looked at him, completely puzzled.

'East is east, dearie – and that's where we've been told to go. What's the problem?'

'Haven't you noticed anything?' Zabad said at last, waving his hand down the valley again. He sounded cross and impatient.

Zilla looked carefully. And then she understood.

'Oh yes,' she said. 'Fancy that.'

She sat down rather heavily on the stone bench beside him.

About a kilometre ahead of them, the valley broadened out and was then blocked by a line of trees. Further east, away on the horizon but clearly visible above the trees, was a bleak mountain, jabbing up like a broken tooth into the sky. Zilla had been aware of these things in the back of her mind for some time, but it wasn't until Zabad made her look properly that she realised what they meant.

The trees could well be the start of a stretch of forest. Their home village of Hazar was in a forest. A great mountain rose to the north of Hazar – it was where The

Dragon of Kiriath had kept its treasure hoard. They were looking at it from a different angle now, but it was certainly possible that the mountain on the horizon was the one Zilla had seen from Hazar every day of her long life. They'd travelled west from Hazar to get to Rakath's castle. For the past few weeks, they'd been travelling back east again. It all added up to one thing.

'It looks as if we're on our way home, dearie,' said Zilla.

'Home for you, maybe,' Zabad muttered.

'What do you mean?' she asked. 'You were born there, too.'

Zabad gave her a hard look, then went back to staring into the pool.

'You can go back,' he said after a while. 'I can't. That's the difference.'

Zabad *was* old, actually, Zilla thought. His hair was grey and thin, his face ploughed with deep lines, his back stooped. He looked in worse shape than you'd expect for a man of his age – she supposed that was the effect of having spent so long working for The Dragon. But despite the signs of age, Zilla couldn't help thinking of him as the boy she'd known growing up in Hazar when she was young herself. She'd carried him in her arms and bounced him on her knee. She couldn't accept that he might remain an outcast.

'You know what the others said,' Zilla told Zabad. 'Now that everyone *knows* why you worked for The Dragon, they can't hold it against you. It's not *your* fault The Dragon didn't kill you when he killed the others who went to fight him. They'd all have done what you did if they'd been faced with the choice of working for The Dragon or being roasted alive. You didn't *want* to work for the thing. You were only too glad when Baladan rescued you.'

It was true. All Baladan's friends had told Zabad that he couldn't be blamed, but it didn't help.

'They may have *said* that,' Zabad replied, 'but did you see their eyes when they said it? It's one thing to say something because it's the right thing to say. It's another thing to believe it in your heart.'

'Don't you think they believed it?' she asked. 'Don't you think *I* believe it?'

They looked at each other for a moment. He remembered the old times in Hazar, too. The beautiful young woman, with hair the colour of sunshine, who'd always had time to play with him when he was a boy. Her hair might be white now and tied up with strange, coloured ribbons, but her eyes were the same – dark grey as the evening sky.

'You're different,' he said.

He got up and walked around, as if he was trying to work himself up to going on but then he dropped back on the bench with a sigh.

'I've spent half my life collecting their crops, their animals, their loved ones to feed to The Dragon,' he said. 'How can I go near Hazar again after that? How could I look them in the face, even if *they* could bear to look at *me*?'

They were quiet for a moment, then Zilla put her hand on his arm.

'You know, *I* don't really want to go back either, dearie,' she said.

He looked at her, surprised, but she was staring at the mountain.

'Because they think you're mad?' he asked.

'What a thing to say!' she said, laughing. 'No, dearie, it's not that. I've lived with that long enough.'

She paused for a minute, as if making up her mind whether to go on.

'It's more to do with the reason they thought I was mad,' she said, at last. 'I spent years keeping Hanan's memory alive when everyone else had given up hope in the things he stood for. He said the King would help us against The Dragon and I hung on to that – I was sure it would happen and that Hanan would be there to see his words come true. Then when Baladan took us to Kiriath and we found Hanan's skeleton, it just knocked the stuffing out of me. I haven't liked to say anything to Baladan – or to anyone, really – but nothing that's happened, even Baladan killing The Dragon, has made up for losing Hanan. No, I don't want to go back to Hazar – there are too many memories.'

'Why on earth did Baladan send us here?' Zabad said, suddenly angry. 'Why couldn't we go north like Ruel and Chilion?'

'Or Thassi,' Zilla chimed in.

'Or down south with Rizpa and Lexa,' Zabad went on, 'or with Zethar, wherever he went. *Anywhere* but here.'

They both stared resentfully at the line of trees at the end of the valley, and the mountain rising beyond.

'But this is where he *did* send us,' said Zilla, after a while.

They were both silent and depressed as, half an hour later, they edged amongst the first of the forest trees. Although she'd lived in it all her life, Zilla didn't like the forest: the gloom, the strange shapes and rustlings all made her jumpy. For Zabad, the forest had become his natural element over the years but he didn't feel any more comfortable in it than Zilla. For so long, he'd slipped in and out of the shadows, striking terror into all the forest villagers as he left The Dragon's demands and took away their sacrifices. Every tree seemed to accuse him of robbery and murder.

As they made their way further in, Zabad felt more and more uncomfortable and he wondered why they both felt bound by Baladan's orders. He supposed that, for himself, it must be gratitude. Baladan had saved him from serving The Dragon, and living with the guilt of the things he'd done had to be better than still doing them.

'Why do *you* do what Baladan says?' he asked Zilla.

'Because of the King,' she said.

'What do you mean?'

'Hanan might be dead,' Zilla told him, 'but I still believe what he said. The King will send help to get rid of every last dragon in his Kingdom. And Baladan's going to—'

'Going to what?'

'I don't know, dearie,' Zilla said, sounding confused, 'he'll just make it happen somehow.'

Zabad was just going to ask if she'd ever heard Baladan say so when a strange sound cut him short. It was the last sound you'd expect in a forest. Not the usual rustling of leaves or cracking of twigs to put you on your guard: this was a clank – a heavy, metallic clank. Zilla and Zabad looked at each other. They knew better than to speak, even in a whisper. There it was again – a clank, and another clank, metal knocking against metal. Then something very heavy hit a tree trunk, and there was a deep growl. The friends had a choice, either to creep forward in the direction of the sound to find out what it was, or to crawl into the undergrowth and hope that whatever it was went away.

They picked the second option but soon realised they might have made a mistake. The sounds were getting louder and were coming in their direction. They were stuck. If they moved now, the thing would be sure to see them. There was nothing for it but to lie still and hope for the best.

Then they saw it. In the early June evening, there was still enough light filtering through the leaves for them to make out the huge man-shaped monster as it stepped out from behind a tree, not twenty metres away. 'Step out' wasn't quite the right description. The monster seemed to shoulder-charge the trunk, making a dreadful clunking noise, then it bounced off and lurched forward, grunting and growling. Peeping between brambles and leaves, Zilla and Zabad saw the thing sway and steady itself. Then it took another step forward, kicked a root and staggered. That was when it made the heavy clanking and they realised that this great monster was actually *made* of metal.

It was as if the creature knew they were there. It just kept coming straight towards their hiding place. Soon they could hear the squeaking and grating sounds it made as it moved. They could see the crude hinges at its knees and ankles, and the rivets holding it together. It wasn't going to stop. It was going to plough straight over them. At the last minute, Zilla and Zabad leapt out of their cover like startled birds and made a run for it. The thing blundered on, tangling itself in the undergrowth before it was able to turn around to come after them. The pair looked back to see if it was following and saw it get its balance, then slowly crane its great cylinder-shaped head forward with a grinding creak. The three of them seemed to be frozen. Then the monster let out a terrible roar. It lurched towards them, and they ran.

It didn't take long for Zilla and Zabad to realise that there was no chance of the monster catching them. In a few moments, they'd outrun it and were so far ahead that they were out of the monster's sight, although they could still hear it furiously clanking in pursuit, crashing into trees and bellowing. The pair stopped to catch their breath.

'We'll have to do something about it,' Zilla said. 'Just because *we* can get away from it doesn't mean it couldn't do damage to someone or something else. It's still a monster. Remember, Baladan said we had to meet the adventures that came.'

'Pity he didn't let us have any weapons to do it with,' Zabad said, holding out his empty hands.

'I've got an idea about that,' Zilla told him, and she quickly explained her plan.

When the monster caught up with its quarries, it only found one victim – Zabad. But it didn't seem disappointed. It gave a triumphant roar – a strange booming, echoing sound, like someone shouting inside a metal box – and came lumbering towards its prey. Zabad didn't turn to run but stood his ground. He tried hard to fix his attention on the great cylindrical head and not to show the monster that he had half an eye on what was happening behind it. It must have looked as if Zabad was paralysed with fear, so he caught the thing completely by surprise when suddenly, with only five metres to go before it reached him, he set off running – not away from it but *towards* it. The monster didn't have time to react before Zabad crashed full tilt into its chest. Zabad dropped to the ground, slipping through the lumbering iron arms, and rolled out of the way. He was in such pain that he thought he must have broken his shoulder, but as he looked up he saw that the charge had done its job. The ungainly thing, rocked by the impact, staggered back a step – right into the crouching body of Zilla. She'd been stalking the monster and had dropped down behind it as Zabad charged.

The monster tumbled over backwards with a crash that set the forest birds screeching. Its legs rose high in the air and Zilla just managed to scramble out of the way before they smashed back down onto the ground exactly where she'd been crouching. If Zabad thought his shoulder was broken, she was sure her ribs were cracked, but she was up again in time to see an amazing sight – the monster's head seemed to have been knocked off and was rolling away into a clump of ferns. She helped Zabad to his feet and the two of them stood there, rubbing their bruises and admiring their handiwork.

'We *did* it!' said Zilla, pointing to the severed head. 'That's the end of him.'

No sooner were the words out of her mouth than there was a deep, rumbling groan and a voice roared out, 'Zabaaaaaaaaad! I'll rip you to pieces!'

The ground was rocky and the two of them armed themselves with boulders. They advanced on the fallen head, meaning to crush the life out of it, but when they reached the ferns, the head was empty – nothing but a hollow cylinder of metal.

'Here, you fools!' the voice bellowed behind them. 'Zabad, you coward, come here so I can kill you!'

They spun round, totally disorientated. The monster's body had started to move. They'd seen the crude sword strapped to its waist and now it had taken this out and was waving it in the air. But most amazing of all, it seemed to have grown a new head – a big, bald, *human* head. Then they recognised it – it was the head of Halak, the village blacksmith from Hazar.

In a flash they realised the truth. The 'monster' was nothing more than a man – Halak the blacksmith – in a very strange suit of armour. What they'd thought was a severed head was just a helmet.

'Halak!' said Zilla. 'What on *earth* are you up to? Come on, let's get you on your feet.' And she and Zabad went to haul him up.

But as soon as they were in range, Halak took a mighty swing at them with his sword.

'I'll cut you to pieces, I swear it!' he shouted. 'I've no

quarrel with you, Zilla, but I'll kill that murdering swine who's with you.'

They were stuck. Halak was like a beetle on its back. He could roar and roll and thrash around as much as he wanted but he couldn't get up. Zilla couldn't shift him on her own and every time Zabad tried to get near, Halak's sword came swinging through the air at him. The only thing to do was leave the blacksmith there but Zilla and Zabad couldn't bring themselves to do that. It wasn't long before it started to get dark and they came to a decision. They'd camp out near Halak in case he needed anything and in the morning, one of them would set out for Hazar to bring help.

Zabad woke to the sound of voices in conversation. He moved then let out a yelp. His shoulder wasn't broken but it was bruised black and blue. The voices paused for a moment then went on. Zabad focused his eyes in the first light of morning. It was Halak talking to someone – and that someone was Baladan. Slowly, and painfully, Zabad stood up. He could see that Zilla was stirring, too, and holding her ribs. The blacksmith was still on his back, where he'd been left, and the two went over to him. But as soon as he saw Zabad, Halak growled and reached for his sword.

'Wait,' Baladan said, grabbing his wrist. 'Remember what we agreed.'

Although he was very tall, Baladan had a wiry body which seemed almost puny next to the great armoured mountain of Halak. But his grip kept the blacksmith's arm from moving.

'All right,' Halak said, at last.

Baladan let go and the blacksmith's arm thudded back on the ground.

Baladan had made a fire. His horse, Hesed, was nearby

and Baladan fetched food and drink from his saddlebags. Halak had never been a great talker so over breakfast, Baladan told Zabad and Zilla what he'd found out from the blacksmith. Halak had made the suit of armour for himself so that he could enter the Tournament, but his skills were in making farming tools so the end result hadn't quite been what he'd intended. Just now, he was trying his equipment out by using it to hunt down a pack of trolls which had been plaguing the village.

'But why on earth do you want to go in for the Tournament in the first place, dearie?' Zilla asked Halak. 'You're a blacksmith, not a soldier.'

'Everybody ought to go,' Halak told her. 'You helped Baladan against The Dragon – everybody ought to help clear out the monsters. Everybody except one.'

'Now come on, dearie,' Zilla said. 'You *know* Zabad wants to fight, too.'

'I'm not talking about him,' Halak growled.

'They've had a visit,' Baladan explained, 'from one of Abaddon's men.'

'Nasty piece of work,' Halak muttered. 'Nobody threatens *me*!'

'What did he want?' Zabad asked.

Halak turned away. He still hadn't spoken to Zabad, or even looked him in the face.

'Tell them,' said Baladan, gently.

Halak pointedly looked at Zilla as he spoke.

'He wants people to fight on his side at the Tournament,' he said. 'He wants the forest villagers to make an army. Free armour if you join him, village burned down if you don't. I told his messenger I'd make my own armour and fight for whoever I wanted.'

'Abaddon's sent his men to Kiriath, too,' Baladan told them. 'Sir Achbor and the other knights there are undecided and the town's in uproar. They've been offered a lot of money.' He turned to Halak. 'Now,' he said, 'it's time to get you on your feet. Remember what you promised.'

The blacksmith nodded.

'Come on, Zabad,' said Baladan. 'He's agreed not to harm you while you're helping him up.'

With that, the three of them levered, heaved and hauled until they'd set the blacksmith back on his feet. Zabad brought Halak's helmet and handed it to him. He snatched it and glared at Zabad with his fierce little eyes.

'The minute I saw you yesterday, I wanted to kill you,' he said, 'and I haven't changed my mind.'

He jammed his helmet on his head with a clang and set off, lumbering and clanking amongst the trees.

'How can he fight in a Tournament in that stuff?' Zabad asked. 'It's ridiculous! He'll never even get there!'

Baladan looked in the direction Halak had taken with an expression that was definitely one of admiration.

'He's determined,' he said, 'and that counts for a lot.'

Zilla had other things on her mind. She couldn't bear to meet up with Baladan without asking after Ruel.

'Have you seen him?' she asked. 'Is he well?'

'Yes, to both questions,' Baladan told her. 'He and Chilion are on their way back south again. They nearly reached the northern border before they turned round. They've been a great help to each other.'

'And the rest?' Zabad asked.

'Thassi and his friends got *beyond* the border,' said Baladan. 'They had to face a dragon up there but they survived. They're heading south now, too.'

Zilla enquired after the sisters.

'They've left the coast,' Baladan told her. 'They're on their way up country and they seem to be enjoying themselves at last.'

'What about Zethar?' Zabad asked.

At the mention of Zethar, Baladan looked sad for the first time.

'He's nearly been drowned and eaten alive and he has more to go through yet,' he told them. 'But he'll be back. He has to be. Everything depends on him.'

They tried to get Baladan to explain but all he would say was that Zethar's mission was secret.

'Are we going to join up again soon?' Zilla asked.

'Not long to wait now,' he assured her. 'We'll spend the summer together.'

At that moment, there was a clattering in the trees like a cartload of armour being tipped over a cliff. It was followed by excited squealing and a deep, booming voice crying out for help. It was obviously Halak. Zilla and Zabad instinctively looked to Baladan for a lead and sure enough, he went to Hesed and drew the great battle sword which hung from his saddle. Its dazzling blade caught the morning light and seemed to make their eyes burn. But then, to their astonishment, instead of gripping the handle ready for action, Baladan held the sword out in both hands and walked up to Zabad with it.

'You do it,' he said, offering him the sword.

The blade was making Zabad's head spin with its brilliance but he found he didn't want to look away. It seemed that Baladan was holding out a pure beam of light and the more Zabad stared at it, the stronger he became. At last, he took a deep breath and grasped the handle of the sword.

'Come on,' he shouted to Zilla, and the two of them set off running in the direction of all the commotion, as fast as their old legs would carry them.

Halak moved so slowly in his armour that he hadn't gone far and they soon found him. He was flat on his back again, helmet off, but this time, his sword had been thrown wide in the fall, leaving him defenceless. He was being set upon by a swarm of tree trolls – nasty, hairy-looking things, half the size of a man but with vicious claws and teeth. Like Zilla and Zabad, they'd obviously found it easy enough to knock over the lumbering blacksmith. Zabad gave a shout and rushed at them, swinging the great sword above his head. He'd picked up some skill at Rakath's castle but Baladan's sword seemed to have a life of its own. It swung and swooped in his hands, making him feel like the finest swordsman in the Kingdom.

Zilla held back, unsure what to do. Then Baladan came up beside her.

'Wait,' he said.

He darted into the mayhem and was back in a moment with Halak's fallen sword. It was more like an iron bar than a knight's blade, but it was still a weapon.

'Here,' he said, giving it to Zilla. 'While you're swinging this, Hanan stays alive. Go to it!'

And with a war cry that stopped even the trolls in their tracks for a second, Zilla charged.

It was a strange fight because neither Zabad nor Zilla managed to strike any of the trolls. They were incredibly agile, dodging and leaping out of the way, but they were clearly not keen on getting near those swishing swords, so between them, Zabad and Zilla were able to drive them away from the fallen blacksmith. At last, the trolls realised they had no chance of reaching their prey so they gave up and raced off, gibbering, into the depths of the forest.

Zabad and Zilla stuck their swords into the ground, shook hands and went to help Baladan heave the blacksmith onto his feet for the second time that morning. But there was a difference now. Instead of looking away from him, Halak kept his eyes on Zabad, with an expression on his face which was impossible to read. When they'd pulled him up,

Halak took Zabad by the shoulders in a crushing grip and fixed him with his tiny, glittering eyes.

'Thank you,' he growled.

Zabad and Zilla went to collect the swords. Halak's was still stuck in the ground where Zilla had left it, but Baladan's was gone. So was Baladan. In the place where Zabad had stuck Baladan's sword, a strawberry plant was growing, its rich red fruit ready for eating.

A deep voice rumbled behind them. 'Help me get home to Hazar.'

They turned back to Halak. He was a sorry sight with blood running down his face and his big, bald head from the scratching of the trolls.

'Yes,' said Zabad.

'Of course, dearie,' Zilla agreed.

But first they gathered the sweet fruit and ate.

CHAPTER SIX

A young boy's voice rang round the village of Hazar. 'It's Halak! Halak's back!' he shouted.

The boy was Ezer, Ruel's nine-year-old brother. He ran the length of the one street in the village and by the time he'd reached the end of it, everyone was out of their houses or coming down from the fields to meet the blacksmith. He was a silent mountain of a man and the children found him scary but all the adults respected him. They'd tried hard to stop him going into the forest after the trolls and they'd been worried about him ever since he'd gone. He was the nearest the village had to its own champion and everyone was glad to see him back.

As he staggered, clanking, down the street from the western end, the villagers crowded towards him but then they stopped in confusion. There was silence for a moment when they saw who he was with.

It was Maaz, Ruel's father, who spoke first.

'Get that man out of here!' he snarled.

There was an angry growl of support from the rest of the villagers.

'Wait, Maaz,' said Halak.

He wasn't wearing his helmet and his deep voice boomed out clearly, silencing them all. The helmet was being carried by Zabad, which was what had pulled everybody up. They'd all heard the truth about Zabad by now but they couldn't help thinking of him by the terrible name they'd had for him previously. To them, he was still 'The Reaper'.

'This man saved my life,' Halak said, putting his hand on Zabad's shoulder. 'He should be made welcome here.'

With that, he continued up the street, Zabad on his right,

carrying the helmet, and Zilla on his left, secretly gripping the elbow of his armour to steady him. Four days wandering the forest in that armour had drained even the huge blacksmith's strength. He was ready to drop.

The crowd opened up to let them through and everyone had a word of welcome for Halak as he passed. But they were quiet words. Zabad's presence had burst the balloon and there was no chance of a party mood. Zabad looked straight in front of him. He didn't bow his head but couldn't bring himself to meet people's eyes and see their expressions. Then he heard his name being called, and he stopped. He forced himself to look to his right and saw Jarib, white hair flowing down his back and white beard flowing down his chest, the oldest and wisest man in Hazar.

'Zabad,' he said, 'you *are* welcome. Come to my house and eat with me.'

Everyone looked at Maaz for some kind of reaction, and Ruel's father felt his jaws clenching with bitterness. He couldn't look at Zabad, but he managed to nod his head and grunt, his best attempt at seconding the welcome. Then he stepped up to Zilla.

'You must eat with us,' he said to her. 'Tell us about Ruel.'

Everyone knew how much Maaz disliked Zilla. He thought she'd filled his son's head with nonsense about Hanan and his message that the King would send help. They knew that for Maaz to welcome Zilla to his house was a huge step.

Baladan had given dragon's gold to the people of Hazar and they had used it to replace their mud-walled cottages with houses like the ones in Kiriath Town, so Zilla sat at a good solid table in a wood-panelled dining room to eat with Ruel's family that evening. Naama, Ruel's mother, was beside herself with fear when Zilla described their winter journey to Rakath's castle but she calmed down when she heard from Baladan's latest report that her son was well. When Zilla described the time spent learning how to fight with swords at Earl Rakath's castle, Ezer dashed off to fetch a wooden sword which Maaz had made him.

'Look, I can do it, too,' he said, making the wooden blade whistle through the air. 'Now Halak's back, I'm going to ask him to make me a metal sword,' he told them, 'then I can go to the Tournament with him.'

Mention of the Tournament started them talking about the disputes at Kiriath about whether or not to support Abaddon, and talk of Kiriath moved to the subject of Ruel's sister, Safir.

'My daughter looks set to be a lady,' Maaz said, proudly.

'She's going to marry Sir Achbor,' Ezer chimed in, 'and he's going to make me a knight!'

Naama tutted sharply. 'We don't know anything of the kind,' she said. 'She's just been helping Sir Achbor manage things in Kiriath. He's had a lot to do since Baron Azal put him in charge of everything.'

'Come on, Naama,' Maaz put in. 'Why else did he send money to Hazar to help us finish our houses? It was for Safir's sake – a token of love.'

'He's just a kind man,' Naama muttered, tidying their bowls away.

<hr />

Next morning, Zilla went to Jarib's house to meet Zabad, who asked her to walk with him a little way into the forest.

'Where are we going?' she asked.

'Somewhere I need to go,' he said. 'And if you don't mind, it would help to have a friend with me.'

Zilla agreed, and they strolled through the trees, blinking

in the shafts of sunlight between the branches and listening to the birds calling. It was going to be a really hot summer. Zabad felt years younger and was walking with a much straighter back. Something had tingled through his body when he'd held Baladan's sword and was still tingling now. He felt as if he had been dead inside since the day, nearly thirty years ago, when The Dragon had captured him, and now, at last, he was alive again. Last year, Baladan had set him free from The Dragon's service but it was only now that he felt he'd been given back his life.

'Yesterday I realised something,' he said. 'You can't wash out the past. It'll always be there. You can't expect people to wipe out their memories…'

'But surely, in time, dearie…'

'No – no, it's all right. That's how it has to be and I've got to deal with it. That's the really important thing that I realised – it was tough walking through those people but I knew I could handle it. I think it's something to do with Baladan giving me his sword, and what we did, and Halak thanking me. It's all made me feel cleaner and stronger inside.'

'I know what you mean,' Zilla said. 'Charging at those trolls seemed to do something for me, too. I suppose you're right – you can't wipe out the past, but there's no point living in it. All my moping over Hanan won't do, you know. It's time to move on. I feel ready.'

It was then that Zilla realised where they were going. Zabad might have said that he was feeling stronger inside but his steps still slowed down as they approached the spot. She found his hand and held it. They were heading for a place he'd been many times before, a place the villagers feared and hated. It was the place where he had always left his signs to say The Dragon wanted another sacrifice. And the place where the villagers were forced to leave whatever The Dragon demanded.

It was only ten minutes walk from the village and soon they reached the little clearing. There was the great fallen log to which the villagers used to tie their living sacrifices, animal or human. And there was the rough pole where Zabad would hang his most dreaded sign, the one which meant death for a Hazar villager. The skull of a pig. Zilla and Zabad stood still and stared at the scene. No bird sang here and no sunbeams seemed able to fight their way through the thick roof of leaves.

They were still holding hands, and their grip tightened then suddenly, Zilla pointed.

'Look!' she said, 'There's something on that pole.'

She was right. Not a skull or any of the other signs and symbols Zabad had used but a scrap of parchment, skewered over the end. Zilla ran and took it off the pole.

'It's from Baladan,' she said. 'It's our instructions!'

<hr>

A fortnight later, Zabad and Zilla were well on their way up the Great North Road and summer had definitely arrived. The sunshine was blisteringly hot and they were soaked with sweat. They'd been walking all morning and could both have done with a rest, but they wanted to push on because they thought they must be near the turning which Baladan had ordered them to take. The Great North Road was an ancient route from a time before their people's history began. It was thought that it ran all the way to the border with the Northern Realm. Right in the centre of the Old Kingdom, the road was crossed by another ancient pathway leading to the border with the Western Lands: this was the route Baladan wanted them to take.

And there it was. They were walking in open country and could see, about half a kilometre ahead, the great standing stone they'd been told to look out for and the course of the western road striking off to the left. The Great North Road kept on going, straight as a spear, until it disappeared over a faraway rise. Zabad and Zilla spotted a small group of travellers, just below the horizon. They looked no bigger than beetles, but the two friends could make out that they were heading south towards them. They'd probably meet up at the crossroads. Zilla and Zabad still had no weapons so they had to trust that these people were peaceful travellers – either that or hide. But they were in no mood to waste time hiding anyway and they would also have been seen by now.

All seemed well until the friends were a couple of hundred metres from the crossroads when the group of travellers started shouting and charged towards them.

'We'd better make a run for it, dearie,' said Zilla, hitching up her gown and turning.

But Zabad stopped her.

'No, wait,' he said. 'Look who it is!'

Zilla screwed up her eyes. The group had reached the standing stone. There were five of them and Zilla realised they were shouting her name. Then she recognised them – Thassi and his friends.

Moments later, the five of them were swarming around Zilla and hugging her.

'It couldn't have been anyone else,' Thassi said. 'When we saw that rainbow gown with a blob of white hair on the top – there can't be another woman in the whole of the Old Kingdom who looks like that.'

'I'm not sure if that's a compliment or not, dearie,' said Zilla.

Then they turned to Zabad. Thassi looked him in the eye for a moment but Zabad didn't flinch. Zabad stuck out his hand. It stayed there for a second or two before Thassi took it firmly.

'How have you been?' he said.

So they sat by the roadside, shared what food they had and started to tell their tales. Zilla passed on Baladan's news about the other groups and told them about the 'monster' which turned out to be Halak. Then Thassi told the story of Oreb the reaver and the runaway prince from the Northern Realm. Zilla and Zabad were keen to hear what it was like over the border. For most people in the Old Kingdom, the Northern Realm was about as real as something out of a fairy tale.

'You should see it,' Hagab said. 'If you thought we had a mountain at home, where The Dragon hung out, you'd better think again! They've got mountains up north that make ours look like a pimple! Loads of them, one after another like walls. You can't even see the tops for cloud.'

'And there's a lot of that,' Saraf put in.

'It just rains for days,' Hagab went on. 'We were all for taking to the caves and waiting for a dry spell, but Baladan said we'd be waiting for ever.'

'He stayed with you, then?' Zabad asked.

'Oh, yes – all the time,' Thassi told him, 'until the end.'

Hagab continued.

'We kept on going through it all until we got to the lad's home. His father was a big chief and wanted to give us presents for bringing his boy back, but Baladan said no, we just wanted to know where their dragon was. So a bunch of their warriors took us on a mountain track to a weird lake, way up amongst the peaks. Then they shook our hands as if they didn't expect to see us again and cleared off.'

'We didn't think we'd meet again, either,' Jaala butted in. 'Not after what Baladan told us to do.'

'This dragon lived at the bottom of the lake,' Hagab went on, 'and Baladan said we had to stand at the edge and wait till it came for us. We were going to be bait. He said if *he* stood there, the dragon would recognise him and wouldn't come out, so we'd have to lead it to him. All we had to do was let it get halfway across the lake to us, then run for it into a narrow gorge behind us. That's where Baladan said he'd be waiting, so once we were there, we could dive behind the rocks and let him do the rest. "Trust me," he said!'

'So did it work?' Zilla asked.

'What do you think? We're still here, aren't we?' Shual said.

'Only just,' Hagab continued. 'You've never seen anything like it. This thing shot out of the water like an arrow the size of a... the size of a... '

'The size of a dragon?' Zilla suggested.

'Yeah, the size of a dragon! It spat out a fireball that rolled right along the water at us. Clouds of steam went everywhere. We dodged—'

'Dodged? Threw ourselves flat, more like,' said Shual.

'Whatever. Anyway, the fireball blasted a hole as big as a house in the rocks behind us then the dragon was coming straight at us out of all the smoke and steam. It was bright green, with a neck like a serpent, and horrible yellow eyes—'

'How come you remember all that?' Saraf asked. 'You were running for it by then.'

'We all were,' said Thassi.

'Just following orders,' Hagab pointed out. 'We led it into the gorge, just as Baladan said, and there he was, waiting for it. We all dived behind the rocks—'

'And some of us didn't look out again until it was over,' Saraf muttered.

Hagab stopped and looked embarrassed.

'You tell them how it ended,' he said to Thassi.

'When it saw Baladan, the dragon pulled up so fast it skidded on the shale,' Thassi told them. 'But then it got its balance and let off another fireball. But Baladan was too fast for it. He took a big jump sideways, drew his sword and charged. Then something weird happened. We were in a cloud up there – there certainly wasn't any sun – but light seemed to pour off Baladan's blade in waves and the dragon started weaving its head about as if it was being dazzled. Baladan was able to get in close before it could spit again and he stabbed it in the chest. Purple blood spurted out and splattered all over him. Baladan must have been blinded because when the dragon swiped at him, he didn't manage to get out of the way and was knocked flying into a big rock.

'Half his jacket was ripped off and you could see a red claw track right down his back. But Baladan wasn't finished. He crawled behind the rock he'd smashed into and kept hidden. The dragon must have thought Baladan was dead because it roared then poked its head round the rock as if it was looking for the body to eat. But Baladan was too smart for it. He'd crept right round the rock and he came out behind the dragon's head, in its blind spot. He jumped on its neck and before the dragon knew what had hit it, Baladan jammed his sword in at the bottom of its skull, right up to the hilt. That was it. The head hit the ground so hard it bounced Baladan clean off it, and the thing was stone dead.'

A rumble of hooves put a stop to the story and when the friends looked up, they saw half a dozen riders coming towards them fast from the west. There was no point in running – they'd have been ridden down in no time – so they leapt to their feet and braced themselves for whatever was coming. They didn't have long to wait: in a couple of minutes, the riders were on them. In a whirl of snorting and stamping hooves, the newcomers drew up their horses in a ring round the travellers and each of them pointed a short spear at the group. All the riders wore a uniform – dark leather jackets, not cracked and old like Baladan's but thick padded jerkins with metal studs. And the fists gripping their spears were protected by studded gauntlets. Short swords hung from their belts and they each had a small round shield hanging at their back.

'Welcome, travellers!' one of them said.

The riders weren't wearing helmets so the friends had a clear view of the speaker's face. A terrible scar ran all the way down the left hand side and his matted hair was pulled back in an untidy pigtail. Several of the friends felt sure they'd seen him before.

'It's not safe to be wandering about in these parts without protection,' the rider went on. 'You need an escort.'

Without waiting for a response, the riders formed up round them – two at the front, two behind and one on either side – and started to herd the friends towards the western road.

'Where are you taking us?' Thassi demanded.

'*Taking* you?' said the rider with the scar. 'This is a *service,* man! Go on alone if you want – but don't blame us if you run into trouble.'

His voice was hard and threatening and he didn't look at Thassi when he spoke.

There was no way out of the tight formation of horses without pushing and shoving and the danger of being trampled. So the seven continued in the centre of their 'escort' as it set off at an easy pace along the westward road.

'What if we don't want to go this way?' Zabad said.

'You'll want to accept the Chief's hospitality, wherever you're going,' the man told him, without looking round. 'It's only polite.'

'Who is the Chief?' Zilla asked, but there was no answer.

Half an hour later, the friends had a fair idea of their destination. The road ran towards a big mound on the horizon and as they came nearer, they could see that it was a hill, high enough to give a view for several kilometres around. At its summit stood a castle. The closer they got, the bigger and stronger the castle looked. It wasn't a fancy place – no flags and gold-covered roofs catching the sun like Kiriath. It was ugly – just a solid mass of dark stone: huge towers with enough arrow slits to cover every angle of attack a dozen times over and wooden fighting galleries at the top of every wall where arrows, rocks or boiling oil could be poured on anyone who managed to get that far. It looked like a place which meant business, a fortress always ready for war.

When the group reached the bottom of the hill, the scar-faced leader gave a complicated signal on a horn. There was a rattle of chains as the drawbridge was lowered and soon the friends were being jostled across it, the horses' hooves rumbling on the wood. When they reached the courtyard, they found a squad of guards awaiting them. The riders clattered off to the stables without a word and the guards immediately surrounded the friends. No answers were given to their questions and none of the guards even looked at them as they were hustled across the cobbled yard, up a flight of stone steps, into the great hall of the castle and on towards the high table on a platform at the far end. It was a gloomy hall, no plaster on the walls, no tapestries, windows the size of arrow slits, and the only person there was a shadowy figure slouching at the high table, gnawing on the rear end of a pig.

When they reached the table, the figure rose. He had Baladan's height with the huge, muscular bulk of Halak and they realised they were looking at the biggest man any of them had ever seen. Filthy black hair hung to his shoulders, and like the riders, he was dressed in studded leather. His head was huge, to match his body. It was the size of a bull's head and it had the round staring eyes of a bull.

When he spoke, the room seemed to shake.

'My name's Abaddon,' he said.

The seven friends were not the only travellers enjoying Abaddon's hospitality. After he had questioned them, they were taken to a smaller hall – a converted store room by the look of it – where they found a couple of dozen more 'guests' of the castle. Most of them were traders, muttering in little groups about the money and goods they'd had to pay Abaddon for safe conduct over his lands. At once, the friends recognised one group, gathered round a table in a corner. Zilla spotted Ruel the same moment he saw her and the two ran to each other and hugged. Chilion strode over to shake hands with Thassi and his group and Zabad went to greet Rizpa and Lexa.

These four had been brought in by Abaddon's riders earlier in the day and had been hoping more of the twelve might turn up.

'We're all here now,' said Rizpa, as the seven newcomers squashed themselves round the table.

'All except one,' Chilion pointed out.

It was then they realised Zethar was missing.

'No one knows where he went,' Ruel reminded them.

'Well, we know somewhere he's *been*,' Lexa said, and she told them about their brief meeting at Lord Zemira's castle and how downcast Zethar had seemed. 'I can tell you what his mission was, too,' she went on. 'He had to *find* something.'

'That makes things a lot clearer!' Thassi said.

'Whatever it is, it must be important,' Zilla put in. 'Baladan told us everything depended on him.'

'Baladan seemed worried for him,' Zabad added. 'He said he'd faced a lot of danger and that it wasn't over yet.'

'But he seemed confident he'd come through it, ' Zilla told them.

When they'd finished speculating about Zethar and exchanged their other news, the friends compared notes on Abaddon. They had all been given the same rendezvous with Baladan but when Abaddon had questioned them, they had instinctively kept quiet about it. None of them had thought it a good idea to let Abaddon know they were going to meet one of his rivals at the Tournament.

'I don't know that he'd be worried,' Chilion said. 'Everyone seems to be backing him for Champion.'

The others agreed. Everywhere they had travelled, Abaddon's men seemed to have been there before them, scattering threats or money or both.

'The thing is,' Thassi said, 'a lot of people seem to think he's the most powerful man in the Kingdom anyway so they're happy to support him *without* the threats. Everyone likes to back a winner.'

'Have you noticed,' Lexa put in, 'there's lots of people who don't seem to mind that he's a criminal? They're just glad of someone who's strong.'

'They want one leader for the whole Kingdom,' Zabad said.

'They want the King,' Zilla put in.

'The trouble is,' Ruel said, 'they don't *believe* in the King, so they're making do with Abaddon.'

There was a commotion at the door and another squad of guards came in, about twenty of them. They lined the walls, hustling the 'guests' into the centre of the room.

'This way,' their leader called out. 'The Chief wants you to see something.'

The friends were marched across the courtyard then through a gate in a wall which cut the inside of the castle in half. The area on the other side of the wall had been set out as a military training yard, where there were men practising sword swings, shield parries, moves with axes, maces, pike, spear, ball and chain. At the far end, a strip had been fenced off and knights with lances were galloping along it at a dangling dummy. There were more men exercising than you could count. An army.

Into the middle of all this strode Abaddon, a head taller than the tallest man in the yard. He drew his blade, marched into the sword practice area and proceeded to take on all comers. Inside five minutes, he'd disarmed the lot and had laid out half of them with the flat of his sword. Then he yelled for a mace and set about the axe men, mace men and even the ones using the dreaded ball and chain. He was incredibly fast for such a huge man. None of them came near him, and one after another, they went down with a kick, a shove or a great slam on the shield from his weapon.

When he'd finished, Abaddon threw the mace away, scattering a group of squires, and stomped back towards his 'guests'.

'You've paid your money, those of you who had any,' he said. 'And tomorrow you'll get what you've paid for – safe passage through the lands I protect. Out of gratitude to me, you'll do me a service. Everywhere you go, you'll tell the people you meet what you've seen here and you'll tell them to come to Earl Melech's Tournament and fight for Abaddon – the man who's going to be crowned Champion of the Kingdom. Make sure you use that word—' he glared at them with his bulging bull's eyes '—the man who's going to be crowned.'

CHAPTER SEVEN

'If that was just an escort, I'd hate to meet Abaddon's men when they're angry,' Ruel said to Chilion.

They had just been run off Abaddon's land by a dozen of his riders and were walking westward with the others on the ancient road from Abaddon's castle to the border. They'd been hemmed in and jostled by the horses, shouted and sworn at by the men and the points of the riders' spears had threatened them all the time. It was a relief to Ruel when their 'protectors' finally sent them on their way with a farewell blast of curses and galloped back to their castle. But Chilion had mixed feelings. In one way, he was as glad as anyone to be out of Abaddon's clutches but in another, it was painful for him to leave the castle so soon. His friend Zethar still hadn't turned up, and deep down Chilion had wanted to stay on until he did. But in the end, they'd had no choice in the matter. Abaddon had shown them as much as he wanted and now he'd turned them out to spread his message on their travels.

The friends tramped on for some time without speaking, each trying to get over Abaddon's rough treatment. It was Rizpa who finally broke the silence.

'I've been thinking,' she said. 'Abaddon said a lot about how he was going to win the Tournament but he missed something out.'

'What was that?' Lexa asked.

'He never mentioned anything about his plans for clearing the dragons afterwards,' her sister replied.

They could still see Abaddon's castle on the horizon behind them but only just. For a few minutes, Ruel walked backwards, squinting at it through the morning haze.

'I wonder if Baladan's castle will be as strong as Abaddon's,' he said.

'What do you mean, dearie?' Zilla asked him. 'What castle are you talking about?'

'The one where he told us all to meet him,' he explained, turning round again and marching with a puffed-out chest. 'We're going to join his army!'

He strutted to the head of their little column and shouted back over his shoulder: 'There'll be twice as many soldiers as Abaddon's, twice as much armour—'

'And he might even give us our swords back!' Thassi muttered.

'One thing's for sure,' Zabad said, 'time's getting on. If Baladan *is* going to enter the Tournament, he'd better be making some preparations.'

Long ago, the western border of the Old Kingdom had been a violent place, bristling with castles. But for generations, the people of the Western Lands had lived peacefully, tucked away in green valleys which led down to the western sea. They'd turned their backs on the borderlands and now the whole area was deserted. All that was left to mark the border between the two lands was a ditch. But it was a big one, deep enough for a soldier to stand up in and still be hidden, and the dug out earth was piled in a huge bank on the western side. It was long too, a couple of hundred kilometres, running the whole length of the border. It was an amazing piece of work and even though it was now overgrown and bits of the bank had fallen back into the ditch in many places, you could still spot it from a long way off. This ditch was the landmark the friends had to look out for. Baladan's instructions were that they should turn south when they reached it then after another day's march, they would come to the castle where he'd be waiting for them.

It took the friends five days to reach the great ditch. Then they turned south, as instructed, and towards the end of the next afternoon, the eleven saw a jagged crag on the skyline. It looked like an eagle about to take off, exactly the description Baladan had given them, but as they came closer, they started to have their doubts that it was the right place. They screwed their eyes up, trying to make out the castle on top of the crag, but they couldn't see one.

'There *is* something up there,' Rizpa said, when they were a bit nearer.

'Only rocks,' Chilion told her.

'No, look – it's not natural. It's some sort of building,' Rizpa insisted.

Chilion looked harder.

'I suppose it could be,' he said. 'But there's one thing it isn't – and that's a castle.'

Everyone had to agree with that.

An hour later, they were at the bottom of the rocky hill and there was no doubt about it – there *was* a building at the top but what *kind* of building they still couldn't make out.

'We'll go up and see if anyone lives there,' Thassi said. 'If so, we can ask if there's another crag like this further south with a castle on it. They're sure to know.'

So they set off, climbing the stony track which wound up the hill. It was a stiff climb and the friends were panting by the time they reached the top. What they found up there surprised them. A big black boulder on a bend in the track made a blind corner, and when they turned it, they stopped suddenly and bumped into each other in confusion. They'd been halted by a wall across the track which had been totally hidden until they came round the rock. There was a little gatehouse in the wall, and although it had no moat or drawbridge to defend it, any force coming round that boulder to attack would find itself suddenly under fire, with no room to manoeuvre and organise an assault. It might not look much from below but whatever this place was, it would be difficult to capture.

Or at least, it would have been in its heyday. The friends soon saw that the wooden door in the gatehouse was rotten and parts of the wall were so badly broken down that they could scramble over them. Chilion followed the wall as it curved away on the right and, a moment later, came back to report a hole that they could simply walk through. However, it seemed good manners to go in by the proper way so, since there was no horn hanging by it, Thassi hammered hard on the wooden door. A lump of wood fell off at the top.

'Hey, steady on!' a shaky voice called out from inside.

A moment later, there was a scraping of rusty metal as bolts were worked back then the door started to move. It had slumped down on its hinges so it dragged on the worn flagstones inside but at last the gatekeeper forced it open and stood barring their way. Bent over with age, he wasn't much taller than Ruel. Wisps of white hair blew round his face.

'Well?' he said, grumpily.

Thassi asked about castles in the neighbourhood but the gatekeeper looked puzzled.

'No,' he said, 'no castles round here – 'cept this 'un.'

'But this isn't a *castle*!' Ruel said, horrified.

The old man straightened up a bit.

'This *castle* ruled all you can see, lad,' he said, fixing Ruel with his watery eyes, 'in its day, that is.'

The friends looked at each other in confusion.

'We're supposed to meet a man called Baladan at a castle near here,' Zabad explained.

The grumpiness went out of the man's face at once.

'Oh, Master Baladan!' he exclaimed. 'You should have said so straight away. Come in, come in!'

The area inside the wall was paved but the slabs were uneven and broken and weeds were growing in between them everywhere. In the middle of this paved area stood the building they'd spotted from the bottom of the hill. They could see now that it was a simple round tower but it wasn't surprising they hadn't been able to work out what it was from a distance. It had a strange, ragged outline, thanks to the fact that bits of the top had fallen off and a big bush had rooted high up there, waving like a sad flag in the breeze.

As Ruel was taking in this scene, he heard sounds which suddenly reminded him of home – the blowing of bellows and the roar of a blacksmith's forge, like Halak's in Hazar. Ruel caught a whiff of smoke then there was a rapid clanging of hammer on metal. These were the only signs of life in the place.

'Come on,' the old gatekeeper said. 'I'll take you to him.'

He led them round behind the tower. A small stone shed was built against the crumbling outer wall and a trail of smoke from its chimney told them that this was the smithy. There was no door and they could see the silhouette of the blacksmith working inside – a dark shadow against a red glow.

'Here he is,' the old man said, leading them straight to the smithy entrance.

Ruel pushed his way to the front and looked in. There, stripped to the waist and shining with sweat in the dim light of the forge, was Baladan the dragon slayer.

Five minutes later, Baladan had drawn a bucket of water from the well beside the tower and was washing away the sweat and grime from his day's work while his friends crowded round him.

'But where's your army?' Ruel was asking, desperately. 'Where are your weapons?'

'All of you are my army,' he said, tossing spray from his wet hair, 'and you have all the weapons you need.'

'Oh, come on!' said Thassi. 'We've been to Abaddon's castle. We've seen his armoury. And there are probably dozens of other hopefuls up and down the Kingdom who've got their forces together. We can't go into a tournament against opposition like that. We wouldn't stand a chance even if we *had* weapons, just you and us.'

'You'll have to hurry up,' Rizpa told Baladan. 'If the Tournament's way over to the east, we'll have to set off in a month. There's men to find and train, and you'll never kit them out working on your own.'

They were surrounding Baladan by the well and they all started talking at once. He held up his hands, laughing.

'Stop!' he said. 'You have to understand something. You need to understand that when it comes to the kind of battles *we* have to fight, it's not what's on the *outside* of someone that counts the most. It's nothing to do with armour and weapons and how well you can use them. It's what's on the *inside* of a person that makes them the kind of warrior I need. You've all been in training ever since you left Earl Rakath's castle. Every adventure you've had has made you stronger people – stronger *inside*. Think of the things you've learned about yourselves – the qualities you've developed. Those are the *real* weapons we need if we're going to put this kingdom right. This—' he jerked his thumb towards the smithy '—isn't about supplying an army. It's a favour for a friend.'

He put on the old leather jerkin they knew so well and led them towards the tower.

'Come and meet him,' he said.

A stone stairway winding round the outside of the tower led to a door about three metres above the paving. Baladan took them up. The door opened into a gloomy room with no covering on its rough stone walls and a simple wooden table in the middle. Two men, their backs to the door, were eating at the table and a third place was set.

'Ah, Baladan,' said the older of the two, without looking round. 'Your food's ready.'

'Sir Bamoth,' Baladan replied, 'allow me to present some friends of mine.'

'What? Visitors?' Sir Bamoth said. 'We're honoured!'

He tried to get up and turn at the same time, and banged against the table. The young man rose, too, and they both came to the door.

'I am Bamoth, knight and custodian of this castle,' the old man said. He glanced at the youth with a proud smile. 'And this is Jalam – my only son and heir.'

Baladan introduced the eleven by name, and Sir Bamoth invited them to the table. Then he remembered that there were no more chairs.

'So long since we had guests,' he said. 'Forgive me.'

He shuffled to the door and stood on the top step of the staircase. He looked as old as his gatekeeper but his back was straighter, his white hair thicker, and even in the poor light, they had seen a sad dignity in his pale blue eyes.

'Ebed!' he shouted in the direction of the gatehouse. 'Fetch chairs for our guests!'

His voice was surprisingly strong and echoed round the little stone courtyard.

Some time later, with help from Baladan and his friends, enough chairs had been found in the cellar, dusted down, tested for rot and carried into the dining room. Ebed had been sent off to find what food he could for the new arrivals.

'My only servant,' Sir Bamoth explained. 'We only need the one, you see.'

'We can only *afford* the one, Father,' Jalam corrected.

'Well, yes, yes – that, too,' the old man agreed.

But he didn't sound put out. He looked at his son with love, and Jalam certainly seemed a young man to be proud of. He was about twenty, strongly built with dark, curly hair and a broad, honest face. His eyes were a deeper blue than his father's and he had the kind of firm gaze which wouldn't flinch, even in front of a king.

'Just think,' the old man went on, 'no guests for – how long? How long since we had a guest, Jalam?'

'I don't know, Father – over a year.'

'Yes, yes, over a year, it must be. And then Baladan. And then all his friends. If you're friends of Baladan's, you're welcome here, you know,' he said to the eleven. 'Yes, yes indeed – we're so grateful to Baladan,' he continued. 'We thought you were only staying the night, didn't we, Baladan? Yes, just offered him food and a night's lodgings out of common hospitality, you know. Then as we were eating, Jalam asked if Baladan had heard of Earl Melech's Grand Tournament. Baladan said he had, and that was it – all the talk was about the Tournament from then on. Jalam's mad for it, you see – can't wait to try his hand. But the trouble is – he has nothing to fight with. Not a weapon or a piece of armour left in the place that's fit for anything – all rusted and rotten.

'It wasn't always like that, you know. This tower was the terror of the district once upon a time. You wouldn't think so, would you? But it was. My family were chiefs of all the land around this place. But that was long, long ago. Half the countryside doesn't even know there's anyone still living here now, I should think. It makes me sad. And it made me sad that I couldn't give my son what he wanted, to go to the Tournament. Oh, I'd found him a rusty old sword and given him what lessons I could but it's years since I last used one. And it's years since our last blacksmith grew too old even to shoe a horse. I pensioned him off and never replaced him.

'As we talked that night, we told Baladan all this, by way of conversation, you know – never imagining he might be the man to solve our problem. But what do you think? Next morning, instead of waving goodbye and setting off on his travels again, he asked to see what was left of the smithy and whatever old gear we still had in the armoury, and straight away he set about mending the bellows and getting ready for work. *He* was going to kit my son out, he said.'

'And now, everything's nearly ready,' Jalam put in. 'And Baladan's been teaching me sword fighting every day.'

'And making a much better job of it than I ever could,' Sir Bamoth said.

'I'll be leaving for Earl Melech's castle soon,' Jalam told them, 'to win the Tournament, and be knighted, and serve the King, and drive out the dragons, and mend my father's house and his fortunes!'

There wasn't a hint of boasting in his voice or in his bright, steady eyes – just a simple eagerness to do good by the strength of his arm. It was easy to see why Baladan had decided to help him.

That night, Ruel had a vivid dream that he and Jalam were fighting shoulder to shoulder at the Tournament. Their armour was dazzling and they cut their way through a hundred enemies until they finally stuck their swords, both together, deep into the heart of Abaddon.

In the days that followed, Baladan set Ruel to work in the smithy. Ruel was amazed how skilful and strong Baladan was. He wasn't built like a blacksmith – his stripped body was wiry and sinewy instead of bulging with muscle like Halak – but he was still able to keep going hour after hour without any sign of tiredness. His back was criss-crossed with scars which showed up clearly through the shining sweat. Most of the marks were pale but one looked raw and new, a reminder of his fight with the dragon of the north.

At last, a special day arrived. Baladan was working on a section of Jalam's body armour, making plates strong enough to stop a sword but light enough to let the wearer move at speed. They had to fit together with precision so that they would slide over each other as easily as parts of a living body and never snag or jam. Baladan heated, hammered and plunged the glowing metal into his vat of water, sending steam erupting all over the shed. Then he put the plates on one side. Ruel had been pumping the smithy bellows, trying to check the colour of the glowing furnace and watch Baladan working at the same time but now Baladan told him he could leave the bellows and watch him finish off the most special job of all. Today was the day that Jalam's sword would be finished.

Baladan had been working on the sword for over a week, laying strips of metal across each other, twisting them together, hammering and shaping them. Each part of the process was long and complicated, and he left some time between the stages, going on to other jobs before he was ready to come back to the sword again. But now it was almost done – a final polishing and it would be ready. Ruel couldn't take his eyes off the beautiful blade as Baladan worked on it in the red glow of the furnace. At last, Baladan straightened up and squinted down the blade one last time.

'Fetch Jalam,' he said.

Jalam came running down the steps from the tower so fast that he nearly fell. Baladan was in the courtyard, waiting for him. The sword lay horizontally across the palms of his hands and he held it out to the young man. Jalam came to a halt in front of him and hesitated. Baladan and Jalam looked into each other's eyes, and there was something strange and solemn in the moment. Ruel hung back, watching from a distance.

'Take it,' Baladan said. 'It was made for you.'

Jalam reached out his hands cautiously, as if he thought the gleaming metal might still be burning hot, and when he finally took the sword he held it out in front of him as Baladan had done.

'Use it,' Baladan told him.

Jalam gripped the hilt and took a few strides away to a safe distance. He raised the sword, took a deep breath, and swung. The blade whistled through the air like a song. It was so light and so perfectly balanced that it almost seemed to fly, and the young man staggered with surprise. Then he found his balance again and took another swing, and another. Soon he was shouting with excitement, sweeping high and low, spinning and leaping as if in a dance, until he was panting and running with sweat. He stopped for breath. Then he saw Ruel, standing in the shadows by the smithy with a real hunger in his face. Straight away, he held the sword out to the boy.

'Here,' he said, 'you have a go.'

Baladan watched with a smile as Ruel took the sword and tried out every move he knew.

'Good,' said Baladan, after a while. 'You learned well at Rakath's castle. Now it's my turn.'

Ruel gave him the sword and Baladan took another look at it – along the flat and along the edge. Then he felt the weight of the weapon for a moment, raised his arm and swung. What happened next was impossible to follow. The blade seemed to disappear into wheels of light as Baladan's arm whirled round his body. Ruel gasped out loud. Then the blade was still again and Baladan was grinning with pleasure.

'It's finished,' he said. 'Use it well.'

And again he held out the weapon to its owner.

Jalam started to thank him but Baladan cut him short and told him to show his father the sword. As the young man ran to the tower, Baladan wandered over to the tumbledown castle wall. He found a stretch to lean on and looked out at the view. Ruel wasn't sure whether Baladan wanted to be alone but there was something he desperately wanted to say. He came and stood close to him for a while, hoping Baladan would turn, but he didn't, so in the end Ruel had to speak up.

'Can Jalam take Zethar's place,' he said, 'and be one of us?'

Baladan looked at him now with a small frown.

'Who says there's a place to be taken?' he asked.

'I don't know,' Ruel said, embarrassed. 'It's just that when Zethar wasn't at Abaddon's, we thought he'd probably turn up here. But we've been here a week now and he hasn't shown up. Perhaps he's not coming.'

'He's not coming *here*,' Baladan explained.

He turned away and looked out over the countryside below. You could see for miles. Ruel thought the conversation was over but then Baladan spoke again.

'Zethar has a very special job,' he said. 'Something only *he* can do. Without him, I couldn't do what *I* have to do. Remember that.'

'I suppose,' Ruel said, after another pause, 'I suppose you *could* take them all on at the Tournament with just eleven of us – and your sword.'

'Could I?' Baladan asked, without looking round.

'Of course you could! Look what you just did with Jalam's sword. With your own sword, you could take on anyone in the world.'

More silence. Ruel was willing Baladan to say 'yes', although he couldn't imagine how anyone, armed with any weapon on earth, could survive with just a small band against someone like Abaddon and his army. But if Baladan said it could be done, that would be enough – he'd believe him.

'Come with me,' Baladan said at last, and he led Ruel to the run-down little stable where his horse, Hesed, was kept. Baladan's sword was hanging on the wall with Hesed's saddle. Baladan carried it out into the sunlight, still in its scabbard, and gave it to Ruel.

'Look at it,' Baladan told him.

Ruel was puzzled.

'I've looked at it before,' he said.

'Look at it and *see*,' his friend told him. 'A sword can tell you many things – by how it's made, what it's made of, how it's used, or not used – or what it *is*. Look at my sword and see what it tells you.'

With his left hand, Ruel took hold of the hilt and with his right, he eased off the scabbard. As it clattered on the broken flagstones, the sun caught the blade and flooded the gloomy little courtyard with brilliant, golden light. Ruel remembered the first time he'd met Baladan over a year ago. The sun had caught his sword then, and the light had exploded in the forest clearing where they were, dazzling him so that he was almost blinded. But the light didn't blind him now, although it seemed incredibly powerful. Instead, it seemed to draw his eyes right into the centre of it.

And in the centre of the light was the blade, but the strange thing was that instead of reflecting light from the sun, the blade now seemed to be *making* the light. The blade was turning into a river of fire: it wasn't that it *looked* like a river of fire – it *was* one! And the river was alive. Every fish you could imagine and every other water creature that exists was in the river and amazingly, they weren't being burned. They were playing and leaping joyfully in the flowing flames. Ruel lost track of time but eventually, his fascinated eyes moved up the blade to the hilt and there he saw that the cross pieces of the guard were formed by the arms of a man and woman, standing back to back, the sword between them. Their bodies were against the root of the blade, their heads against the base of the hand-grip and their outstretched arms were clasped together by the hands. They were dressed in rags but on their heads were shining golden crowns.

The hand-grip itself was a tree trunk, wound round with creepers. Every creature that lives on the earth was running up and down the trunk and every plant was springing out from the creepers. Every known flower was blooming and every fruit hung there. More than that – all the fruits and flowers of the different seasons were growing at the same time. Last of all came the ball at the end of the hilt. Every flying creature in the whole world was circling round it, humming, buzzing and singing for all they were worth. The ball itself was the whole universe. Ruel saw the moon and the stars and planets. Comets whizzed past. Suns flared up and died away.

As Ruel gazed in wonder, whole ages seemed to pass. His head swam and he felt himself being sucked into the hugeness of space where stars were scattered as thickly as snowflakes in a storm.

There was only one thing holding him back. Somewhere a voice was talking to him, saying his name. It was a voice from long ago and far away – someone he thought he'd known. He struggled to remember. And then, at last he had it and hung on to it – it was Baladan.

'Ruel,' he was saying, 'Ruel, now do you see?'

And slowly Ruel realised that he was standing on broken paving stones in the summer sunshine, with Baladan's sword in his hand. The scabbard had been slipped back onto it and Baladan was taking it from him. Ruel felt strange and slightly sick, the way you do when you've been spinning for a long time then stop.

'Jalam's sword is for tournaments,' Baladan told him. 'What you had in your hands is not for games.'

Baladan took the sword back into the stable and when he returned, a bewildered Ruel had another question for him.

'I've been thinking,' he said. 'When everyone told each other about their adventures, they all said you'd met up with them?'

'So I did,' Baladan replied.

'You must have moved fast, even with Hesed,' Ruel went on.

Baladan said nothing.

'And according to Lexa and Rizpa, you were with them at the same time Thassi says you were fighting the dragon of the north. You were at different ends of the country at the same time!'

Baladan didn't deny it. Ruel gaped at him.

'Who are you?' he asked, and his voice came out in a whisper.

'What did the sword say?' was all that Baladan replied.

CHAPTER EIGHT

ethar watched a formation of little birds swooping over the cliffs. They joined up into a big flock then headed out to sea. Autumn was on its way and they were going wherever they went for the winter. Living in the forest all his life, Zethar had never before realised that these little creatures went away across the sea. What *was* there over the sea? How brave they were, heading out into nowhere! Not a scrap of fear in them. Fear was of great interest to Zethar. It had been on his mind all year – it was the thing Baladan had sent him off to find.

'Find your fear,' had been Baladan's instructions, 'then come to me at Earl Melech's castle.'

On his own, and with no orders about direction, Zethar had had every part of the Old Kingdom in which to look. He had searched north, south, east and west but now, as the year took the first steps towards its end, he was no nearer success than when he'd started. The little birds, wheeling in the skies then making off for the horizon, seemed to be making fun of him. They had a whole world left to travel in, but in the south-eastern corner of the Kingdom, Zethar had come to the end of the road.

He found a way down to the bottom of the chalky cliffs and wandered about on the beach for a while. He felt that he needed to wet his feet in the sea to prove to himself that he could go no further, that the whole thing was ended and that he hadn't found what he'd been sent for. Or maybe he *had* found his fear and just hadn't realised it. As he scuffed around on the sand, clambering over rocks, he thought over the worst moments of the last six months to see if any fear was hiding in his memories.

Zethar remembered a time in the early spring before he'd met up with Lexa and Rizpa. Rain had been falling heavily for days and he'd been tramping up to his ankles in mud along a river bank in a long wooded valley. The river was very full, right up to the top of its banks, and the pale brown water was running so fast that it made him dizzy if he looked at it too long. The dizziness, the river's noise and the hissing rain made Zethar confused and slow to react. As he struggled on, mud sucking down his feet at every step, he became vaguely aware that there was an extra unidentifiable background noise but he couldn't focus on it properly: all his attention was on the muddy track at his feet.

It was there that he saw the first signs of danger. The river was no longer flowing beside the track. It was flowing *over* it. Zethar scrambled away to the slightly higher ground on his left but as soon as he reached it, the water seemed to be coming up after him. It was only then that the strange background noise forced itself into the front of his mind. It was a roar, deeper than the sound of the river and the rain, growing louder all the time. Suddenly, it was very loud and coming from one clear direction – behind him. He turned just in time to see something rush round a bend in the valley, about half a kilometre away. It took a moment for him to make sense of what he was seeing – but then he knew. It was a wall of brown water, frothing and foaming like beer pouring out of a huge jug and surging towards him.

His heart thundered and he was away, running and scrambling up the valley side. But the wall of water was too fast. Like a line of cavalry, it charged him down. The noise was deafening and the force of the wave threw him as if he were no bigger than an acorn. Every bit of him was concentrated on fighting to the surface and getting breath. Again and again he succeeded, only to be dragged back into the water and have to struggle yet again. From time to time, his body was jarred as it banged into heavy branches but he was freezing and felt no pain from the blows, only the breath being knocked out of him and more water choking his lungs. He was being carried through the tops of trees and sometimes he became stuck. Branches smashed as he wrenched himself free, struggling back to the surface.

Then suddenly, it was over. The water was still carrying him at speed, but the roaring destruction of the first flood wave had passed on down the valley. Now his head was above water; he was swimming. He was alive. The ridge marking the top of the valley was still above water and Zethar struck out for it. Soon he was back on solid ground, panting and retching, but safe.

As he stood on the beach, sea water lapping at his feet, Zethar wondered if he'd found fear in the flood all those months ago. He looked out over the waves and examined his feelings. No, there'd been no fear – only a pounding heart, powering his body up for action.

It had been the same up by the borders with the Western Lands as spring had turned towards summer. He'd woken in the middle of the night to hear an animal rooting about in his belongings. It had obviously smelt the food in his sack and was becoming angry because its paws weren't made for the job of undoing leather thongs. In the moonlight, Zethar soon saw why. They were made for slashing and smashing and they belonged to two and a half metres of brown bear.

Like everyone else, Zethar had handed over his sword to Baladan but in the first town he had reached after leaving

Rakath's castle, he'd taken work with a builder until he had earned enough money to buy himself another sword. It was a clumsy, battered weapon but it did its job when Zethar took a firm grip and without a second thought, plunged it straight into the bear's chest. He had felt no fear, only surging energy – and anger when the creature fell forward, the sword still sticking out of it, and snapped the hilt clean off as it hit the ground.

Zethar had acquired a replacement sword by the time he reached the north in midsummer. It was better quality than the one the bear had broken and it needed to be. Late one afternoon, Zethar was on his way toward a little village tucked in the shadow of menacing-looking peaks, when suddenly, the sound of hooves came drumming fast from the track behind him. He turned and saw two bare-headed riders, in padded leather jackets, thundering towards him. Zethar stood aside and the men rode straight past, but as they did so, one of them leaned down and took a swing at Zethar's head with his hand. He was wearing heavy, studded gauntlets and knocked Zethar flat.

'Abaddon for Champion!' the rider shouted over his shoulder.

Zethar scrambled back to his feet again, fuming.

'Losers!' he yelled.

The riders reigned in their horses sharply and brought them to a halt. Armed with short spears, the men came charging back at Zethar, obviously intending to skewer him, but he leaped sideways so that only one could lunge at him. With a quick slash of his sword, he lopped the head clean off the rider's spear. That angered the man, and he jumped from his horse, drawing his sword. The other rider turned to charge again but now that his friend was so close to Zethar, fighting hand to hand, he couldn't attack. While the man was still on his horse, wondering what to do, Zethar held his position. He managed to cut his opponent high up on the left arm and thought he might even stand a chance of winning until the second man decided to dismount and join the fight. After that, it was obvious in seconds that Zethar had no chance but he didn't give up and run. He concentrated totally, using every trick he'd learned at Rakath's castle as well as a few more he came up with on the spur of the moment, before they finally hacked him down.

However, the riders were prevented from finishing Zethar off by the arrival of people from the village. They weren't keen on strange riders in their neighbourhood, and they certainly weren't prepared to see two men with horses attacking one man on foot. Someone had given the alarm and a dozen villagers quickly arrived on the scene, swinging staves and scythes. If they'd still been on their horses and fresh, the riders might have fought them off but Zethar had done damage to both of them before he went down and it was all they could do to fight their way back to their mounts, scramble into the saddle and head off down the track.

'Abaddon for Champion!' they shouted, from a safe distance.

Zethar heard one of the villagers send a volley of curses after them, then he passed out. He was in a bad way. A slash across the back of his thigh had felled him and before that, one rider had managed to slice into the side of his chest. The villagers thought Zethar was done for but they took him to the village where one of their wise women treated him with herbs and bandages. At first, she held out little hope but as the days passed, and Zethar writhed and raved with fever, she began to think there might be a chance.

'Look at him,' she'd say to anyone who came to see the stranger. 'He just won't give up!'

And it was true. The fever couldn't break him. The higher it rose, the more he seemed to clench himself and wrestle against it, until finally it was the fever, not Zethar, that broke.

***

It was towards the end of summer before Zethar was mended and back in the middle of the Kingdom, on his way down south again. It was there, just west of Earl Melech's lands, that he had the strangest experience of his journey. He had camped on top of a low hill and had bedded down in a clump of trees. There was a broad clear area on the summit of the hill, with an ancient circle of stones standing like a ring of sentries. Just as dawn was breaking, Zethar was awakened by something happening amongst the stones. It was a mixture of chanting and some sort of horn-blowing and there was a terrible stink.

Zethar crept to the edge of the trees to see what was going on. The dew was turning into mist and was lying close to the ground at about waist height across the hill so the people making the noise looked as if they were just floating half-bodies. If that was strange, so was their clothing. They were all wearing flowing white gowns with hoods shading their faces, like some kind of uniform. Zethar had never seen anything like it. They were dancing in time to the strange sounds and waving their arms about.

Zethar would either have stayed where he was or just slipped away if there hadn't been a sudden scream from the middle of the group. It was a woman. Zethar had never needed much of an excuse for a fight and Baladan had told them all that they must accept any adventures which came their way so he was up on his feet immediately, running towards the stone ring. Then he realised he wasn't the only one who had been watching what was going on. Other men must have been hiding in the trees because Zethar found he had four companions beside him, racing across to the circle, waving staves.

One of them seemed to be the leader.

'Let her go!' he bellowed.

The rest yelled battle cries as they ran. The chanting stopped suddenly as everyone in the circle turned to face the charge. Zethar was surprised that no one seemed to be preparing to fight. No weapons were drawn and the people simply stood there, waiting for their attackers. He could see now that there were about a dozen of the white-robed figures in the ring.

Zethar guessed that his four companions must be some sort of rescue party so he took his lead from them and when they pulled up at the edge of the circle, he did the same.

'Let her go!' the leader shouted again but his voice didn't sound quite so defiant now. Although it was still quite misty, Zethar could see better now he was close to the scene. Most of the figures were in a circle and in the middle was one man, standing by a stone table. On either side of the table fires were burning, creating the stink as well as adding to the misty effect. Zethar couldn't begin to guess what was burning on the fires but the smell seemed to be a cross between a filthy pigsty and a week-old sheep carcass.

Through the haze, Zethar could just make out a teenage girl, also dressed in white, lying on her back on the stone table. It was obvious what was happening. The man by the table was holding a big, curved knife above the girl, ready to strike.

But he didn't use the knife to attack the rescuers. He just held it out and pointed it, like a long metal finger, at the man who'd shouted. Zethar and his companions gasped as, with his free hand, the man slowly drew back his hood to reveal a skull.

The skull began to chant. The other men in white joined in with its deep sound from under their hoods. The chanting seemed to shake the earth. It was no language Zethar had ever heard but it had a dreadful effect on the four men. They started shaking and whimpering like dogs. Their leader, making a massive effort, raised his stave to charge into the circle but he didn't seem able to move a step forward. Then the others tried to run away. They twisted on the spot but it was as if their feet were chained to the ground. They couldn't move. The chanting became louder and the men's whimpers turned into moans, then the fires suddenly exploded into shooting columns of coloured flame – green, red and yellow. The moans became shrieks and the four men collapsed, writhing on the ground. The girl on the table was writhing and shrieking, too.

Zethar felt very strange. His head was swimming as if he'd drunk too much beer. The sword in his hand was starting to feel very heavy. He felt it jar his wrist as its point hit the ground then suddenly he gave his head a great shake and jerked his arm up again. It took all his strength.

He swore violently and threw himself at the man with the knife.

The man stood his ground, chanting for all he was worth, pointing the knife at Zethar's chest. Two men with horns started blowing them continuously. Zethar swung his sword at the knife, sending it cartwheeling out of the man's hand, and at the same time smashed his left fist into the skull face.

It shattered. It was nothing more than a clay mask. The man put his hands up to the bleeding human face behind it and started a high-pitched wailing. The other men in white joined in and those with the horns threw them down.

Zethar ran round the table, kicking the fires to bits, then charged at the circle of men, swirling his sword above his head and roaring. The men all turned tail and ran, their leader with them. Immediately, the four rescuers and the girl stopped their shrieking and writhing and lay still. Zethar went to untie the girl and found, to his surprise, that there was nothing holding her to the table. The girl sat up, blinking in the morning sunlight.

'Who on earth are they?' Zethar asked her.

'They're the Wizard Kings,' she said. 'They rule our land.'

'Not any more they don't,' Zethar said.

The four men were struggling to their feet, shaking their heads and looking dazed.

'You ought to throw those wizards out,' Zethar told them. 'They're no better than dragons, having sacrifices like that!'

***

So Zethar had travelled on south until he reached this place, the farthest corner of the Old Kingdom. And here he was, kicking up sand, listening to the swish of the sea, watching the little birds leaving him behind as they disappeared towards the horizon. He had to admit that he had failed. He'd been though the worst that bullies, beasts, nature, sickness and sorcery could throw at him and had found no fear in any of it. He would have to return to Baladan empty-handed. Angry and disappointed, he started to make his way back up the cliff.

***

A few days later, Zethar was deep in a forest as thick as the one where he'd grown up. It made him think of the time last year when he and Chilion and the others had been wandering in that forest back home, trying to find Baladan. They'd been completely lost. But there was no wandering around this time. He was keeping to a direct line north and he had known from childhood how to use the signs of the forest to keep a straight course. Travel north for one more week, then slant off to the east. That would bring him to Earl Melech's lands, just as autumn started. He would wait there for Baladan and the others and admit his failure.

In the middle of the day, Zethar spotted light ahead. The trees were thinning and he thought he was coming to the edge of the forest. But when he emerged from the trees into pale sunlight, he realised he was in a huge clearing. He could see the solid wall of trees at the other side of it, about a quarter of a kilometre ahead. That dark wall curved gently towards him on either side until it eventually joined the treeline from which he had just come. And in the middle of this gigantic tree-ringed arena was an enormous mound of rock. He couldn't make out details at a distance but it seemed to be grey, ancient rock, covered in great patches of lichen – dull yellows, pale greys, dark and dirty greens. The rock was as tall as a castle tower and shaped like an upturned bowl. On his travels, Zethar had seen a few rocks like this – they looked totally out of place, as if they'd just dropped out of the sky, but he'd never seen one anything like this size.

Zethar was hungry so he sat at the edge of the clearing to eat a little bread and cheese. In all his journeys, he had never taken charity. He'd earned everything. This food was payment for an hour's work splitting logs at the last village he'd visited. As he chewed his bread, he remembered the axe head, smashing the logs apart. It had felt good. It always felt good to use his muscles and to see the effect they were having. As his mind wandered to other times when he'd felt that kind of satisfaction, his eyes stayed fixed on the huge stone lump in front of him and as he looked at it, he started to have a vague feeling in the back of his mind that there was something wrong about it. The feeling grew stronger and stronger until he was concentrating all his attention on the mound.

What he saw surprised him so much that he spoke out loud.

'It's moving,' he said.

It was ridiculous. Rocks didn't move. Zethar screwed his eyes tight shut, then blinked several times, hoping to clear his vision. But the rock still seemed to be moving, pulsating gently as if it was breathing.

'Trick of the light,' muttered Zethar.

Nevertheless, he drew his sword and started to walk slowly towards the mound.

When he'd covered about half the distance, he was brought to an astonished halt. Suddenly, the whole thing heaved upwards. It seemed to twist and roll slightly, there was a deep rumble like a sigh in the depths of the earth and for a heart-stopping moment, Zethar caught sight of a huge leg which had been tucked away beneath it. Then the surface of the mound shifted. It was an enormous wing! It had been lying flat against the body of a dragon so huge it made the Kiriath monster look no bigger than a cow. In the moment that Zethar realised this, the dragon raised its head. The neck had been curled away on the far side, out of Zethar's sight, but now it reared up into the sky and twisted in his direction. As it did so, the monster yawned. Its head was the size of a small house and its gaping jaws, swinging down towards Zethar, seemed to blot out the sky.

Blackness – deep, dark, empty blackness – was what Zethar saw in the Great Dragon's mouth – eternal emptiness, universal nothingness, complete extinction of everything. It was vast beyond imagination: emptiness without borders or bottom, endlessly spreading, sucking in every spark of light or life, every pulse of energy that had ever existed. Zethar felt as if he'd been turned inside out, as if he was staring into a dark, empty universe inside himself then falling into it. A dead weight of darkness, dropping through darkness, invisible, falling for ever.

'The next thing I knew, I was lying flat with trees all around me,' Zethar said. 'I was in the middle of the forest again, and by the light, it looked like early evening. I must have been running for hours. I could hardly breathe and my legs were like jelly. I realised I didn't have my sword. I looked around but couldn't see it anywhere. Maybe I'd thrown it away. All I could remember was the dragon yawning. I don't think it even noticed me before I ran.'

He was talking to a beggar he'd met on the road. It was a week since he had seen the dragon and Zethar was close to the place where he would have to turn east to Earl Melech's castle. The two had been walking together for an hour and had stopped by a stream to drink and rest. The beggar had seemed to know that something was troubling Zethar and had asked him what it was.

Zethar had leaped at the opportunity to talk. Ever since encountering the Great Dragon, he'd been desperate to share his experience because he didn't understand it. Never before had he run from anything in his whole life. If he hadn't run, the thing would have eaten him. No way could he have fought it. But what did that matter? The likely outcome had never had any effect on his behaviour before. The previous year, when Baladan had led the twelve up the Kiriath Dragon's mountain, Zethar had been first to follow Baladan on the last climb to The Dragon's cave.

There was something about the beggar, the quiet way he listened and nodded, that helped Zethar explain all this to him. The beggar's face was hidden by a ragged hood, which seemed to help, too. Zethar didn't think he could bear to look someone in the eyes and say what he was saying.

'Most people would think running away from a dragon was a sensible thing to do,' the beggar said, when Zethar had finished. 'Why does it worry you?'

'I've told you,' Zethar replied, impatiently. 'I don't *do* that sort of thing.'

'But *why* don't you?'

The question brought Zethar up short. He'd never really considered it before. Maybe because the answer seemed obvious. Running away was cowardly. But as he thought of saying that to the beggar, he realised it wasn't the right reason. Zethar knew that he didn't care about being cowardly or not.

When it seemed that Zethar was not going to answer his first question, the beggar tried another.

'Have you ever felt that way before?' he asked. 'The way you did when you saw inside the dragon's mouth?'

It looked as if Zethar would not answer that question, either. There was a long, long silence. He knew that he *had* had that feeling, years and years ago when he was a child. Had he the courage to search his memory and find out the cause?

The beggar put out his hand and laid it on Zethar's. Normally, Zethar would have pulled away but now he let it be. And in that moment, he succeeded in his quest. He saw himself in the village of Hazar. He was six. He was staring at his father. His father was squirming, twisting and screaming in a way that didn't sound human. It was taking four strong men to hold him. The lots had just been drawn and he had been chosen to be sacrificed to The Dragon.

Losing his father had been terrible. But nothing in the experience had been worse than that struggling and screaming. It wasn't that he was ashamed of his father. Why *shouldn't* someone scream at a time like that? Why *shouldn't* someone try to run from a dragon? It was sensible – the beggar had just said so. It was the horror of seeing a human being reduced to such a state that had stuck in Zethar's heart all these years.

'It's fear which frightens me,' Zethar said, quietly. 'It's fear that makes everything black and empty.'

Later they set off again and the beggar took Zethar to a causeway which led eastwards over a stretch of boggy fen.

'That's the way to Earl Melech's castle,' he said. 'Four days' journey.'

Without a word, Zethar turned east. He was like a sleepwalker. The beggar continued on his way northwards. A cold gust of autumn air caught his cloak as he walked away. It flapped open for a moment, giving a glimpse of a cracked leather jerkin, but Zethar didn't see it.

CHAPTER NINE

arl Melech's lands in the east of the Old Kingdom were almost completely flat – acres of low, watery fields, fens, reeds and mud – but Baladan and his eleven friends had found one of the few hills and camped on it. It was more of a mound than a hill, but it gave them a view for miles in every direction. Further to the east, half an hour's walk away, they could see a much bigger mound with a wide area of more solid ground around it. On top of this stood Earl Melech's castle but the castle didn't interest Baladan. Ever since they'd arrived, he'd been keeping watch over the road which led in from the south-west. Every day it was bustling with people, as were the roads from the west and north, and they were all going towards the castle. The leaves on the sparse trees were turning to royal colours – red, yellow, orange and gold. Breath was visible, autumn was here and so was the Grand Tournament. For days, people had been arriving in small groups, large groups, groups resembling small armies, and Baladan had been watching them all.

Now there was only one more day to go before the Tournament began and as usual, Baladan had taken up his watch with the first light of dawn. Midway through the morning, he suddenly put up his hand to shade his eyes.

'Chilion!' he called.

Chilion was with him straight away.

Baladan pointed to the south-west road.

'Go and fetch your friend,' he said.

Chilion screwed his eyes up. Sure enough, he could make out a single figure amongst the groups coming in from the south-west, but he couldn't tell whether it was a man or a woman, let alone whether it was Zethar.

'How do you know it's him?' he asked.

'Go and get him,' Baladan repeated.

Baladan had equipped his friends with tents and when Zethar made his way up their hill with Chilion later that morning, he was encouraged to see a business-like encampment. The tents weren't as colourful as many of those spread out on the plain between them and the castle – just dull brown canvas with no pennants fluttering from their poles – but Zethar preferred the look of Baladan's tents: the dark colours suited his mood. The other eleven had gathered to greet him and he looked around the little band with something like pity in his heart. They had no idea what they were up against and he didn't know if he could tell them.

'Where are the others?' he asked Baladan.

'What others?' asked Baladan.

'Your army – are they camped down there?' Zethar pointed to the city of tents, covering the plain in front of the castle.

'There *is* no one else,' Chilion said, quietly.

Zethar looked from face to face, trying to understand, but everyone was staring at the ground.

'So we're just going to pitch in and hope for the best,' Zethar suggested. 'All right – Baladan can still win. It's the best fighter who'll be chosen as Champion – he doesn't have to be in the winning army.' Still none of the friends would look him in the face and he saw that they were all unarmed.

It was Ruel who found the courage to explain.

'Zethar, it's not going to *be* like that,' he said. 'We're not going in for the Tournament.'

Zethar stared at Ruel and a wave of panic flooded him.

'Then what are we doing here?' he said. He turned to Baladan. 'Have you come here just to watch?'

'We came here to meet you,' Ruel explained.

'Then what?' Zethar asked.

'That's up to you,' Baladan said.

'Us?'

'No, Zethar – just you,' Baladan told him. 'You're the only one who can make this turn out the way it must.'

Zethar shook his head as if a cloud of flies were buzzing round it, making his long hair fly in all directions. Ruel realised how matted and messy it was.

'You *must* kill the Great Dragon,' Zethar said, clenching his fists.

'Yes,' Baladan replied, quietly.

'So you have to enter the Tournament.'

'Why?' Baladan asked.

'Because you're going to need an army – the biggest army there's ever been – and they'll only give you one if you win the Tournament.'

The tone of desperation in Zethar's voice shocked his friends.

'What's happened to you?' Chilion said quietly.

Zethar stood still and shut his eyes but they immediately jerked back open and he shook his head wildly again. Whenever his eyes closed, he saw the great darkness of the gaping jaws. Briefly, in stumbling words, he told them about the vast monster he had encountered.

'It *must* be killed!' he insisted.

His eyes were flickering from one person to the next and Ruel thought he looked mad.

'This Tournament isn't the way to kill the Great Dragon,' Baladan told him.

'Why not?' Thassi asked. 'What other way *is* there?

Zethar's right – if the dragon is as big as he says, you'll need an army.'

'It's not the way,' Baladan explained, calmly, 'because this dragon can't be killed with weapons, no matter how big an army you raise. No one can fight it and live.'

'Not even you?' Ruel asked softly.

Baladan looked at him and didn't reply. Ruel was shaken. Baladan was the most confusing person he had ever met, but deep down, in all the time he'd known him, he'd never thought there was anything Baladan couldn't do.

'So you *won't* fight the Great Dragon?' Zethar asked, and the words sounded like an accusation.

Now it was Baladan's turn to close his eyes but unlike Zethar, he kept them closed a long time and bowed his head.

'I will meet this dragon,' he said at last, his voice so quiet they hardly heard it. 'And when the time comes, I'll meet it alone.'

It took a moment for this to sink in but then everyone realised what it meant.

'You *can't*!' Rizpa burst out. 'It'll kill you – what's the point?'

Suddenly everyone was talking at once, all agreeing with Rizpa. Baladan kept absolutely still, his head down, and they closed in round him in a clamouring ring.

'We won't *let* you!' Rizpa cried above the rest.

Baladan looked up suddenly at this, his eyes blazing.

'Do you want to *save* the Great Dragon?' he said. 'If it isn't destroyed, the reign of the dragons can never be ended.'

The power and anger in his voice silenced them.

'We want to save *you*,' Lexa said, gently.

There were streets between the tents. As groups had arrived for the Tournament, they had camped together in blocks and the spaces between the blocks had turned into pathways through the tent city. Smaller bands and individuals had found larger groups to join, and slowly the armies which would face each other in the Tournament had started to form. It was a reasonably friendly process – after all, it was how well you fought, not which side won, that was the most important thing, and everyone was going to have to fight together against the dragons in the end. It was friendly – except for Abaddon's men.

Abaddon's leather-jacketed ruffians were everywhere, stomping up and down the streets in squads. The leader of each squad had a scroll of parchment with names on it. The squads were tracking down all those who'd said they'd fight for Abaddon and hadn't yet come to pitch their tents in his camp. Earl Melech's own men were overseeing the whole thing, trying to make sure the fighting was saved for the Tournament, but they missed some nasty moments as Abaddon's men 'dealt with' people who had changed their mind about their promise.

Abaddon himself was making sure he was out and about. Most of the people gathered for the Tournament had only ever heard of his reputation but had never seen him in the flesh. Just seeing his giant body, with its great bull head, was a powerful persuader for most people not to stand against him and Abaddon knew it.

With only one day to go, Abaddon was making an extra effort to gather every last bit of support. He was spending time meeting new arrivals, trying to steer them towards his camp. That morning, he'd stationed himself on the road from the south-west and just before noon, his big eyes brightened as he saw two new arrivals walking their horses in file towards tent city. It was the leader of the pair who had attracted Abaddon's interest. His horse was unusual – big and strong enough for war, but pure white and graceful in its movements like a horse bred for the hunt. There was something strange about the knight's armour. It was fine and sparkling, obviously of high quality, but like nothing Abaddon had ever seen before. It was highly decorated, as if it came from another age, and the main plates were covered in swirling patterns of inlaid gold. Abaddon was sure it must be worth a fortune and his mouth watered like a dog ready for its dinner.

'Welcome,' Abaddon boomed out, as the riders came close.

They halted and the man in the fine armour raised his visor. Abaddon was surprised to see a very young face with bright blue eyes and orange hair.

'Earl Melech?' the knight enquired.

The big man laughed and took hold of the horse's reins.

'Not quite,' he said. 'I'm Abaddon.'

The knight looked startled and tugged at the reins, trying to free them.

'Unhand my horse, peasant!' he cried.

Abaddon seemed to swell like a toad. He tightened his grip and pulled the reins, making the big horse stagger towards him.

'*What* did you call me?' said Abaddon.

He spoke quietly but there was such menace in his voice and his staring eyes that the knight's face went as white as his horse.

'You are speaking to the Lord Zemira,' he said, trying to steady himself. 'The Lord Zemira does not deal with thieves and – and peasants.'

Abaddon knew he could lift Zemira clean out of the saddle but the anger in his bulging eyes suddenly turned into a cunning little twinkle. He'd spotted something in a bag hanging from the horse's saddle. It wasn't anything he ever had a use for in his own castle but he knew what it was – a minstrel's harp.

'Fond of a song, are you?' he asked, nodding towards the bag.

'Ballads,' Lord Zemira said, huffily, 'stories of chivalry and love.'

Abaddon bowed his head to hide a smile.

'I have a story,' he said. 'It might be the kind of thing you're interested in. All about a man robbed of his birthright. And a wise woman's prophecy.'

Lord Zemira brightened and he turned in his saddle to the rider lurking behind him.

'Come, Sir Shamma,' he said. 'Here may be a tale worthy of your attention.'

As Lord Zemira's companion drew up to them, Abaddon took notice of him for the first time. He saw that he had a decent enough horse, dark brown and strongly built, but as for armour, it was ridiculous: just a collection of scrap metal.

'What's that?' Abaddon asked.

'My friend, the noble knight, Sir Shamma,' Lord Zemira informed him. 'He has met with so many dangers and misfortunes on his way that when I found him he was horseless. I have been able to provide him with a steed but nothing on earth will persuade him to exchange his armour. It seems he has taken a vow.'

Shamma was still wearing a bucket for a helmet. He took it off now, showing a tangle of white hair, tousled with the sweat of his morning's ride, and fixed Abaddon with his watery eyes.

'Abaddon!' Shamma announced. 'Your fame goes before you. All the land speaks of you and I am here to make my challenge.'

He tugged at his sword hilt and after a brief struggle, he

managed to free the rusty old weapon from its scabbard, waving it in the air and setting all his armour clanking.

'Yours will be the first head to fall to my blade,' he cried.

'I'd better have you on my side, then,' said Abaddon, not flinching.

'Never!' the two riders replied together.

'That's not very polite,' Abaddon went on, sounding hurt. 'You haven't heard my story yet – it's about me.'

Lord Zemira seemed a little softened by this.

'Even a peasant deserves courtesy, I suppose,' he granted. 'Say on.'

So Abaddon told his tale. He positioned himself between their horses and as he spoke, he took their bridles, leading them slowly in among the tents towards his camp. Imagination was not Abaddon's strong point, and as the story was a pack of lies, he was rather hesitant over it but it seemed to him that a few long pauses only made the yarn sound more genuine. The point of his tale was that he was not really a swineherd's son but a knight from an ancient, noble family whose inheritance had been stolen by evil sorcery. There had been a prophecy at his birth that he was born to save the Old Kingdom from dragons and monsters. Abaddon felt particularly proud of that touch.

'So you see, gentlemen,' he finished, 'the only decent thing to do is to support me. A true knight has to help someone in trouble – isn't that right? And it's written in the stars, twigs in the fire, dregs in the beer, anything you care to look at, that Abaddon must save the Kingdom.'

He'd been telling his story with his head bowed but now he faced his listeners and drew himself up to his full height. He fixed them both with staring brown eyes and twisted their reins in his huge fists until the horses snorted and struggled.

'Well?' he said.

'Well,' Lord Zemira replied, 'it seems your case is unanswerable. How say you, Sir Shamma?'

'Aye, my lord,' the old man agreed.

They both looked considerably relieved to have an excuse to join the huge man after all.

'My camp!' Abaddon announced, pointing to the tents they'd reached. 'Good to have you aboard.'

He came round behind the horses and slapped their rumps. They set off amongst the tents so quickly that Shamma was nearly thrown from the saddle. Abaddon watched them go, a grin on his face. He felt pleased. He was used to bullying people to get what he wanted; it made a pleasant change to fool them instead.

'Pair of idiots!' he muttered, and marched off back to his station, savouring the prospect of the fortune Lord Zemira might be worth.

<hr />

As well as streets between the tents, odd spaces had also developed where people could gather. In one of these, a group of competitors were listening to a man dressed in a studded leather jacket. They all knew he was one of Abaddon's men. They would probably have told him to clear off but he wasn't alone: the group was surrounded by about a dozen leather-jacketed thugs.

'As soon as the Tournament's over,' the speaker was saying, 'the army must take control of the Kingdom.'

A big man with a shining bald head butted in. He had been creasing his face so hard in an effort to understand that his tiny eyes had almost disappeared.

'I've come here because of the dragons,' he said. 'Nothing to do with controlling kingdoms.'

'Me, too,' said someone else, and others agreed.

'The dragons come later,' the speaker told them. 'First we have to make sure the Kingdom's safe – and Abaddon's your man for that.'

'He hasn't won the Tournament yet,' the bald man pointed out.

'*Whoever* wins that Tournament, Abaddon's your man. Am I making myself clear?' The speaker stared hard at them all and the ring of leather jackets moved in closer. 'He's the only one strong enough to do the job,' the man went on.

'Baladan can do it!' the bald man protested. 'I've come to join *him*. Where is he?'

There was an awkward pause and the ruffians looked to their leader to see what they should do. After a moment, the man's hard face broke into a smile meant to look understanding.

'Good question,' he said. 'Lots of people are asking it. And the answer's obvious – wherever he is, he's not *here*. If we're going to fight the dragons, the Old Kingdom needs a strong army and a strong leader. The army's here. Abaddon's here. Baladan's not. You might *prefer* to fight for Baladan but you haven't any choice. Simple as that.'

He put his hand on the bald man's shoulder for a moment then nodded to the squad and they moved off about their business, spreading the message of Abaddon, the army, and controlling the Kingdom throughout the camp.

Halak stared after the leather jackets and brushed his shoulder as if the man's touch had left some dirt there. He could have fought them all but he couldn't fight the argument they'd just put to him. The group he'd been with drifted apart, muttering that maybe they'd better support Abaddon after all. Halak went back to the handcart which he'd dragged all the way from Hazar. In it was piled his armour and under it, he had been sleeping. People kept giving it and him strange looks. In the middle of all these crowds, he felt very lonely, uncertain and far from home.

Back at the edge of camp, Abaddon was checking on the road which led in from the north. He was glad he had gone there because he'd met a man after his own heart, something which always put him in good spirits. The man, sitting on a tough little pony, told Abaddon he'd ridden all the way from the northern border. When Abaddon asked if he could count on his support in the Tournament, the man told him he didn't work for people.

'What *do* you work for then?' Abaddon asked.

'Money, friend,' he replied. 'It's something you can trust!'

Abaddon laughed and the rider joined in.

'I've plenty of that,' Abaddon told him, and digging into the leather pouch at his belt, he held out a handful of small gold coins. 'Do we have a deal?'

The man took the money.

'There's more?' he asked.

'Lots more.'

'As long as it keeps coming, I'm your man,' the rider told him.

'I like you,' Abaddon said. 'What's your name?'

'Oreb,' the man answered.

'Hey!'

The shout came from behind Abaddon and he swung round. Then he heaved an irritated sigh. About fifty metres back, among the tents, a small troop of armed men was marching towards him. They weren't one of his own squads: they wore the blue surcoats of Earl Melech's men and at their head was a young knight with a marshal's yellow plume bobbing on his helmet.

'What do you want *now,* Achbor?' Abaddon asked, in a weary voice.

'I *saw* that,' Sir Achbor told him.

'Saw what?'

'Money changing hands. The rules of the Tournament state that no bribery—'

'The rules of the Tournament! The rules of the Tournament!' Abaddon repeated in a mocking sing-song. 'You know, you're really starting to get on my nerves, boy. I seriously suggest that you dump that equipment Melech's given you and join my camp, otherwise, if I come across you in the Tournament, I'll make paste out of you!'

The council of knights at Kiriath had argued long and hard about whether to join Abaddon and at last they had decided against it. On the journey to Earl Melech's lands, Sir Achbor had worried constantly about the decision but once he'd arrived and met Abaddon, every doubt had died on the spot. He'd met Abaddon many times over the past week. Thanks to Sir Achbor's connection with Kiriath and his friendship with the legendary Baladan, Earl Melech had welcomed him as a hero; and the Earl had appointed him as one of his marshals, giving him special responsibility for keeping an eye on Abaddon. This had turned out to be a nightmare job. Every time Achbor came across Abaddon, he seemed to be up to no good. But there was always one threat that could keep him in check:

'Breaking the rules means disqualification from the Tournament,' Sir Achbor reminded Abaddon. 'I shall have to make a report to Earl Melech, and... '

'What are you going to report, friend?' Oreb broke in. 'That a man was repaying his debts?'

Abaddon gave the reaver a puzzled look.

'Did you enjoy the shipment of wine I sent you?' Oreb asked, giving him a wink.

'Oh – oh yes,' Abaddon said, getting the idea. 'Very fine.' He grinned at Sir Achbor. 'Why don't you come and have some with me?' he said. 'You know you're always welcome in my tent.'

Sir Achbor didn't reply. He simply drew his men up in formation and stood in front of them with his arms folded, watching Abaddon and Oreb. Abaddon looked from Achbor to Oreb and back again, fuming.

'What are you staring at?' he demanded.

There was still no answer from Sir Achbor and no movement.

At last Abaddon growled, spat and stormed off towards the western road.

Oreb watched him go with an amused smile. Then he turned to Sir Achbor.

'I hope you've said goodbye to your mummy, son,' he told him, 'because that man's going to have you, whichever side you're on.'

And, trotting past Sir Achbor, he disappeared among the tents.

In the early afternoon, Abaddon saw a lone horseman coming in from the west. If your life amounts to nothing much more than fighting, you get an instinct for picking out a serious enemy at a distance – it's a matter of survival. As soon as he saw this knight, Abaddon knew he meant trouble. He couldn't have said what it was exactly – the way he sat his horse, perhaps, but it was more than that. As the man came closer, there was something about the whole of him – the way he held his body and every move he made – that said: 'Watch out.' Then there was the armour – nothing fancy, just straightforward strength and quality.

Abaddon had wanted Lord Zemira with him because he couldn't bear to give up the chance of getting his hands on his money. He wanted this new arrival on his side because something told him he couldn't afford not to.

The knight was riding without his helmet and as he came nearer, Abaddon could see that he was young, probably no more than twenty, but this didn't make him feel any easier. The rider's deep blue eyes fixed on Abaddon's without the slightest hint that he was intimidated by the giant man standing in his path. Abaddon drew a breath to give his usual welcome but the newcomer beat him to it.

'Where's Baladan?' he asked. 'I've come to join his camp.'

Abaddon was taken aback and it was a moment before he remembered his stock answer.

'He's not here,' he said, at last, 'or ever going to be.'

'Oh, really,' the young man replied, coolly. 'Why not?'

'You've been listening to too many stories,' Abaddon told him. 'He doesn't exist, that's why. He's a legend, a myth.'

The young knight drew his sword. Abaddon instinctively reached for his own but then saw the newcomer wasn't making ready for a fight. Instead, he squinted down the blade and turned it this way and that.

'He makes a pretty good sword,' the young knight said, 'considering he's a myth.'

'What?' Abaddon gaped stupidly.

'Baladan made this,' the knight told him. He sheathed the sword again and touched his breastplate with his gauntlet. 'And this armour,' he said. 'Now tell me where his camp is.'

There was no point in denying there was a camp of Baladan's supporters in tent city. The young knight would find out soon enough. It wasn't a big camp but it was the one thing which worried Abaddon about the coming

Tournament. Nothing he or his leather-jacketed men had been able to do or say had shaken these stupid, stubborn people. Despite the fact that none of them had ever seen Baladan, despite the fact that most of the Old Kingdom seemed able to believe Abaddon's tale that Baladan and the Kiriath Dragon was just a children's story, they were adamant that Baladan was real and they were going to fight for him. Now here was this youth, claiming he'd been armed by the wretched dragon slayer. That had to rank as the second worst thing that could happen. The worst, of course, was that Baladan himself would turn up to lead the camp that was rallying round his name.

Abaddon knew that he ought to drag the lad off his horse and kill him there and then. But he also knew it wouldn't be a clean job. He'd not be able to finish him off without a real fight. It would be noisy. People would notice. He looked quickly over his shoulder and cursed. There was that idiot Achbor and his troop again. If bribery was against the rules, doing away with the opposition before the Tournament started was sure to be.

'Look,' Abaddon said, quickly, 'Baladan's not here and he's not going to be, sword or no sword. The Kingdom needs a strong leader. You need to fight for him. Let me introduce myself. I'm—'

'You're Abaddon,' the young man said, impatiently. 'I guessed. My name's Jalam. Now show me to Baladan's camp or get out of my way.'

chapter ten

It was getting dark. Zethar knew he'd have to make a move soon, one way or the other. All afternoon, he'd been sitting alone at the bottom of the mound where Baladan was camped. Chilion and Thassi had been to talk to him, as had Zilla, but he had said little to any of them and they hadn't been able to persuade him to join them. Ruel had asked Baladan why he didn't speak to Zethar himself but Baladan had said it was best to leave him alone.

Camp fires were being lit in tent city. Zethar could see them flickering in the distance and could just catch the faint sound of singing, laughter and drums on the evening air. Over there among the tents was life and light, and in the middle of it was the mighty Abaddon – certain to be Champion, certain to lead the biggest army the Old Kingdom had ever seen against the Great Dragon. Zethar looked over his shoulder to Baladan's little camp. If a fire had been lit, he couldn't see it. No sounds came from the tents: no army here, no weapons, even. No hope.

A broad flat area stretched between Baladan's camp and tent city. It was on this open ground that the Tournament would begin in the morning. As night fell, the round harvest moon shone on a figure marching quickly across the plain towards tent city. He was walking so fast you might have thought someone was chasing him but no one else was on the move. It was Zethar.

As he came closer to the tents, the sounds grew louder. The fires were crackling and there was a clanging and scraping of metal cooking pots and dishes. Fiddles, pipes and drums were being played. Zethar could hear bursts of cheering and shouting and the jabber of excited talk. Clearly no one was intending to prepare for the Tournament by having an early night. Zethar crept among the tents, darting glances to right and left, looking over his shoulder every few steps.

It wasn't long before he saw what he was searching for – a gang of tough-looking men in leather jackets. They seemed to be taking a break from scaring people and were gathered round a beer barrel, enjoying a drink with a group of Earl Melech's blue-coats. The excitement of tomorrow had set off a carnival atmosphere in tent city and everyone was having a good time – everyone except Zethar. Looking at the laughing faces of the men, Zethar felt a complete outsider. After a moment, he stepped up to the nearest leather jacket.

'Take me to Abaddon,' he said.

The man stared at him for a second, trying to focus. He was obviously drunk.

'Great man, Abaddon,' he drawled, 'gonna be king of the army – gotta be strong – kingdom needs a – what was it?' He turned to his friends for help.

'Oh, forget it,' one of the other leather jackets told him. 'We've had enough of that for one day.' He turned to Zethar.

'Big striped tent up there on the right,' he said, pointing. 'Red flag with a gold crown and sword on it.'

It was a big tent, right enough, but Abaddon seemed to fill it. He was slouching in a wooden chair, the trestle table in front of him spread with diagrams of attack manoeuvres. Half a dozen of his lieutenants were in the tent, too, but they all seemed to have finished planning for the night and were halfway through a barrel of wine when Zethar was shown in.

The robber chief looked Zethar up and down for a moment as if he were a piece of livestock.

'Now, what can we do for you?' he asked, his brown bull's eyes finally settling on Zethar's face. They seemed to bulge even more after the drink.

Zethar stared straight back.

'Are you going to kill dragons?' he asked.

Abaddon smiled. He picked up a pewter drinking cup and squeezed it in his huge fist until it squashed like clay. Wine squirted all over the place.

'Nothing easier!' he said.

Everyone roared with laughter – but not Zethar.

'I want to join you,' he said.

Abaddon spread his arms wide.

'Welcome aboard,' he said. 'Better late than never! Are you on your own or have you got friends? Who are you with?'

'I'm with Baladan,' Zethar replied. '*Was* with him, I mean—'

Abaddon straightened slowly in his seat and turned to his lieutenants.

'Out!' he ordered, waving his huge hand.

They went without a word.

'*Right* out!' he bellowed and the vague shadows which could be seen through the tent fabric melted away.

'Now,' he said, beckoning Zethar nearer. 'Tell!'

Zethar gave him an edited version of the facts. He, Zethar, had had a brush with a monstrous Great Dragon and was determined to see it dead; he'd joined Baladan because he'd already proved he could kill dragons but Baladan wasn't going to enter the Tournament and didn't seem to have any plans for fighting the Great Dragon so he'd left him.

'You're *sure* he's not going to enter the Tournament?' Abaddon asked.

'Positive,' Zethar told him.

'And he doesn't want to fight this Great Dragon?'

Zethar hesitated then told Abaddon about Baladan's strange suggestion that he would somehow 'meet' the Great Dragon on his own.

'But that's ridiculous,' he said. 'It'll just kill him and that'll be the end of that.'

'Yes,' said Abaddon. 'So it will. Where is he?'

When Zethar told him, Abaddon went quiet. He stood up, stooping to keep his head from scraping the roof of the tent. He walked about for a few minutes then put a hand on Zethar's shoulder.

'I've got an important job for you,' he said. 'Will you do it?'

'Tell me what it is,' Zethar replied.

Abaddon leaned closer and Zethar was enveloped by the reek of stale wine and sweat.

'If Baladan plans to meet the Great Dragon, he'll need to know where it is,' he said. 'Take him to it.'

Zethar felt as if someone had tipped ice down his neck.

'I told you – it'll kill him,' he said. 'What's the point?'

'The point,' Abaddon told him, 'is that there are people at this Tournament who want to follow Baladan. I'm not stupid. Even when the Tournament's over and I've won, even when they're in my army, they'll *still* want to follow Baladan. I can't have him suddenly turning up and taking half my army away. What if we were on our way to fight the Great Dragon ourselves and Baladan split the army? You see what I'm saying?'

Zethar nodded.

'As long as he's alive, he's a threat,' Abaddon went on. 'If you want your Great Dragon dead, you'll have to finish Baladan first.'

Abaddon went to a wooden chest in the corner of the tent and brought back a small canvas bag. It clinked as he held it out to Zethar.

'Will you do it?' Abaddon asked.

The shouting and singing and the camp fires were dying down by the time Zethar made his way back across tomorrow's battlefield. People had obviously decided they needed *some* sleep before they fought each other next morning. Halfway back to Baladan's camp, Zethar stopped and opened the bag Abaddon had given him. He tipped the coins inside it into his hand and looked at them for a moment. He closed his fist on the money and gripped tight till it hurt, then he suddenly jerked his arm and flung the coins high into the air. As they flew, they caught the moonlight and fell in a shower of silver into the grass behind him.

Squeaking wheels, creaking timber, shouts and cracking whips woke many of the contestants next morning. Teams of men and horses were hauling four huge viewing platforms, one for each of the Great Earls of the Old Kingdom, from the shadow of Earl Melech's castle out to the corners of the Tournament field. Later that morning, each earl, with ten wise councillors, would take his place on one of the platforms and from there, these teams of judges would watch the fighting and pick out the most skilful warriors.

After the noise of the platform-building came the rumble of carts. Contestants were starting to stumble out of their tents, squinting with blurred eyes to see what the commotion was. The carts were piled high with timber stakes and teams of workmen were running along beside them. As soon as the platforms were anchored in place, the workmen started throwing stakes from the carts and hammering them into the ground to mark out a boundary for the Tournament field.

In Baladan's camp, the friends had a good view of the preparations. Ruel, the first up, watched it all. He saw the great boundary ring completed, the striped canvas roofs put on the viewing platforms and the flags identifying each earl's place. There was Earl Melech's blue with a yellow star in the centre. Then Ruel recognised the red and green quartered flag which had flapped in the winter wind over Earl Rakath's castle, far in the west. Over one platform, there was a pure white flag with a gold border and a golden sun in the middle. Rizpa and Lexa had told Ruel they had come across these colours on the south coast, worn by the men of Earl Jamin who ruled in those parts. Ruel himself had seen the fourth flag when he and Chilion had travelled in the north – it was purple with a silver eagle. They had seen it fluttering from the lances of a squadron of Earl Zafon's cavalry.

By the time the sun had cleared the morning mist and the earls and councillors had taken their positions, everyone in Baladan's camp was up. Silently, they watched the shining stream of warriors flow out of tent city and form a dense ring round the boundary, ready to cheer the others when they themselves weren't fighting. On their mound, Baladan's twelve stood apart from one another, each burning with the same thought.

Ruel spoke for them all when he turned to Baladan.

'Can't we go down?' he asked. 'Just to watch.'

At that moment, Baladan actually looked more miserable than all of them put together.

'That's for you to decide,' he said.

Ruel looked round at his friends and saw they were all watching him.

'Come on then, dearie,' Zilla said.

The pair of them set off down the gentle slope and one by one, the others followed until there was only a single figure left on the mound – Baladan. He watched them for a few minutes then he turned away and started packing up the tents.

───────

The roar from the crowd was ear-splitting and the ground shook under Ruel's feet as the first two lines of cavalry charged each other. When they met, the sound was like a hundred suits of armour being thrown at a stone wall – the most tremendous crash Ruel had ever heard. It took him some time to make sense of what had happened. Horses without riders were galloping everywhere. Those with riders were wheeling round ready for another charge and scores of fallen knights were struggling to climb back on their feet before they were mown down. Blunted weapons were being used in the Tournament. People weren't supposed to be killed – after all, they would eventually be needed to fight the dragons – but a great deal of damage can be done when someone is pitched off a warhorse at speed in full armour. Quite a few men who went down made no attempt to get up again. One of them Ruel recognised as Sir Shamma. His bucket had rolled away and he lay unconscious, his head on a pillow of white hair. A few more men hobbled to the barriers, knowing they were finished for the day – ribs cracked, arms broken or shoulders dislocated. The injured were automatically out of the Tournament but in addition, any contestants who were knocked down and had their helmets pulled off by an opponent were counted as 'killed' and also had to retire.

Another couple of charges and most of the knights were on the ground. Then there was a trumpet blast and another deafening roar – not from the crowd this time, but from the two armies of infantry as they raced across the field at each other. If the cavalry meeting had been the biggest crash Ruel had ever heard, it didn't hold the record for long. Those two masses of armoured men running into each other made such a huge noise that it sent Ruel dizzy. As the hundreds of men swung and hacked at each other's shields and armour, yelling out in rage or pain, the din just went on and on.

It was impossible to speak and be heard. Zilla was standing next to Ruel, and he wanted to ask her who she thought was winning but it was pointless. The two armies battling it out were Abaddon's men and an army made up mostly of warriors from the north. It looked to Ruel as if Abaddon's forces had the upper hand. During the cavalry charges, Abaddon had stayed on his horse, knocking down three of the opposition. But he'd followed the rules and dismounted when the infantry joined in and Ruel could see him clearly now in the thick of the fighting. He was wearing armour – as were all his leather jackets – so he couldn't see Abaddon's face but he was clearly recognisable, standing head and shoulders above anyone else in the battle.

The din didn't prevent Zilla trying to communicate. She poked Ruel and bellowed at him, pointing at the heaving mass of bodies. He couldn't make out what she said, but looking where she was pointing, he saw an extraordinary sight. A metal giant – not as big as Abaddon but still a considerable size – was wading through the packed mass. Fighters were aiming blows at him but they just bounced off and twice Ruel saw swords break on the strange armour he was wearing. It was made of crude, thick plates with none of the careful shaping and hingeing of a normal suit but it still allowed the giant to swing his arms and with each swing someone crumpled. Zilla was still screaming at Ruel and at last he realised what she was saying – she was yelling out the name 'Halak'.

Ruel couldn't believe it. If it *was* Halak, he seemed to be fighting on *Abaddon's* side. Whoever he was, the metal giant was very unsteady on his feet. Several times, Ruel saw him stagger but the crush of bodies held him up. It was only when the fighters suddenly thinned out around him that a mace blow on the back of his strange cylindrical helmet sent him reeling. He crashed to the ground and the man who had felled him tugged off his helmet, revealing the unmistakable bald head of Halak the blacksmith.

Ruel wasn't the only one of Baladan's friends to have a surprise when they saw someone they recognised fighting for Abaddon. Lexa shook her sister's arm and pointed out an ancient, highly decorated suit of armour which neither of them would ever forget. A lady's red favour was wound around the helmet, rather lopsided, thanks to the fall Lord Zemira had had in the first charge. But he'd managed to scramble back to his feet and now he was being buffeted about on the fringes of the fighting. He seemed confused, continually suffering whacks and glancing blows, and spinning round swishing his sword at thin air, as if swatting flies. It seemed to the sisters that he was only surviving because none of the opposition was concentrating on him long enough to finish him off. It couldn't last. Everyone was out to impress the judges with as many 'kills' as possible and a burly northern knight eventually flattened Zemira with one blow of his war hammer. He pulled off Zemira's helmet, releasing a cascade of orange hair, and the defeated lord staggered off to the edge of the field, looking very relieved that, for him, the Tournament was over.

No surprises for Thassi and his friends, however, when they saw the man who had obviously been given the job of defending Abaddon's back. His helmet had no visor so they had no difficulty recognising Oreb, slashing and thrusting with deadly efficiency. He and Abaddon were still together, fighting fiercely, when a blast on the trumpets signalled the end of the contest. It had lasted just over half an hour. The northern army had been forced right to the edge of the field and Earl Melech, as chief judge, had decided that enough was enough. Everyone who remained unconquered on the field formed up in lines in the middle and the four earls, with their councillors, went up and down the ranks giving red ribbons to those they had marked out as the best fighters, the ones who would therefore progress to the next round. Abaddon held his ribbon high in his fist and a cheer went up from his supporters. When the robber left the field, Oreb was at his side, a red ribbon in his hand, too.

⚜

The next contest was the army of Baladan's supporters versus an army made up of 'neutrals'. This was a much closer contest and went on for nearly an hour before the trumpet blast put an end to it. Earl Melech judged that the two sides had fought themselves to a standstill. Ruel made two identifications during the fighting. One was a knight wearing a lady's favour round his helmet which looked like the pale brown girdle from his sister Safir's dress. If it was, there was only one knight who could be wearing it but it was only when the contest was over and the visors lifted that Ruel saw his guess was right. The knight was Sir Achbor of Kiriath. The other warrior he picked out didn't need to raise his visor to be identified – Ruel recognised the armour because he'd seen it made. It belonged to young Jalam. Both Achbor and Jalam fought for Baladan's supporters and fought well. They each left the field holding a red ribbon.

And that was the end of the first round of the competition. Everyone who wanted to fight had now had the chance and two hundred warriors had been chosen to enter the next round. The contestants went back to tent city to eat and tend their wounds and the two hundred who were to fight again were given time to rest and repair their armour as best they could.

It was early afternoon before the clarions called everyone back to the action and the remaining competitors were drawn up into their battle lines. From this clash, two supreme warriors would be chosen by the judges to meet in a final single combat to decide the Champion.

It was obvious how to organise the two sides. One was made up of Abaddon's supporters, the other consisted of Baladan's people, with anyone else who was not for the robber chief. Abaddon and Oreb were in the middle of their battle line; Jalam and Sir Achbor had taken up the lead positions for the opposition. A single trumpet blast and the fight was on – no cavalry this time, just two hundred men in steel, running at each other as fast as they could go. When they met, some of them even bounced with the force of the impact. As soon as they hit the ground, they crawled clear and made their way sadly to the boundary – in this round, anyone who went down for any reason was out of the contest immediately.

The smaller numbers and the stricter rules thinned out the contestants more quickly, so this contest was much less chaotic than those in the first round. It soon developed into a series of single combatants or small groups fighting it out. Abaddon's force was better organised and obviously working to some kind of plan but the opposition were holding up well. Then Abaddon made his move. He'd spotted the heart of the resistance – round Sir Achbor and Jalam – and with Oreb at his side, he started smashing his way towards the pair.

With his first blow, Abaddon bashed the visor clean off Sir Achbor's helmet. Blood scattered from his nose as he shook his head to clear the dizziness and Abaddon laughed out loud when he saw who he was fighting.

'I said I'd paste you,' he bellowed through the holes in his visor. 'Make sure you play by the rules now!' And he swung his sword up towards Achbor's crotch.

Sir Achbor was just in time, bringing his shield down to protect himself and knocking Abaddon's sword sideways. Both of them spun round with the force they'd used and ended up facing away from each other. Achbor threw himself backwards with all his strength, barging into the huge robber and sending him staggering. Achbor had hoped that would give him time to wheel round and catch Abaddon before he'd recovered but the big man was incredibly quick on his feet and when Achbor turned, he found the robber's sword already swinging towards his head. He ducked just in time but with his back swing, Abaddon smashed his elbow down onto Achbor's helmet and sent him sprawling. He was out of the contest.

Abaddon didn't waste time gloating. He quickly looked round for Oreb but couldn't see him. Parrying blows automatically, he scanned the fight then saw the reaver. He was fighting hard and had been driven far away from his master. His opponent was Jalam. Oreb never used a visor and although he wore more armour than his usual breastplate, he still seemed half dressed next to Jalam's full suit of steel. But he was so fast that Jalam hadn't been able to finish him off. His short sword and small round shield blocked everything the young man could throw at him. But neither could Oreb land a decisive blow on Jalam. Oreb found himself continually on the defensive and it seemed that Jalam might end up driving him right out of the fight.

Suddenly, Jalam seemed to lose his concentration. He dropped his guard, letting Oreb catch him on the side of the helmet. Jalam stayed on his feet, but bent over swaying, as if stunned. Oreb took a stride forward and raised his sword high over his head, ready to bring it crashing down on Jalam's bowed head and finish him. But the instant Oreb committed himself, Jalam suddenly lunged forward, still bent. There was no turning back for Oreb. His sword came down into the space where Jalam's head had been, just as that head powered into Oreb's belly. Oreb doubled up over the young man's back and when Jalam jerked upright again, Oreb's legs left the ground and he went flying, landing in a winded heap on the ground.

A moment later, the trumpet sounded and the contest was over. Twenty minutes' furious fighting had been enough to leave only about fifty fighters still on their feet, more of them on Abaddon's side than against him. The remaining competitors leaned on their weapons, panting, while all the judges met to consult. It didn't take them long to agree. Earl Melech marched up to the warriors holding two golden ribbons, the passports to the final bout. He gave one to the all-conquering Abaddon. The other went to Jalam.

Abaddon and Jalam were allowed an hour for rest and repairs then they stepped into the ring for the third and last time that day. All the other contestants who could still stand were gathered round the boundary. Most of them couldn't see the fight but just wanted to be there. There was complete silence in the crowd as the two contestants stood in the centre and held their swords crossed. Earl Melech was with them, their swords resting on the tip of his – then with an upward sweep of his blade, Melech parted their weapons, there was a great roar from the crowd and the final began.

At the beginning, the fight looked completely one-sided. Abaddon was so much bigger and more powerful than

Jalam that he seemed to be driving him all over the field. No one had caused the giant serious trouble for the giant all day and it looked as if this contest would be no different.

But the strange thing was, Abaddon didn't seem able to finish it. The minutes went by and although Abaddon was landing blow after blow, Jalam was still solidly on his feet. He was taking most of the hits where he wanted them – on his shield – and was getting in a few in reply. The big man began to slow up noticeably. He'd begun by raining blows in a frenzy but soon he settled to the steady rhythm of a forester who knows he has to hack through a massive tree trunk.

It had been a long day's fighting and exhaustion was setting in. After fifteen minutes, the contestants separated and stood apart, resting on their swords and breathing hard. When they started again, it was Jalam who lifted his blade first. He seemed to catch Abaddon half-asleep and the big man only just raised his shield in time to ward off the blow that came swishing towards his head. And he didn't quite recover quickly enough to stop Jalam following through by barging into Abaddon's chest with his shield. The robber went staggering backwards. Jalam seemed to realise that it was now or never because he instantly threw down his shield and, taking his sword in two hands, launched himself at Abaddon. The sudden fury took Abaddon completely by surprise and all he could do was parry the hail of blows. For the first time that day, he was in retreat.

But he held on. Jalam threw everything he had at him. The big man staggered and tottered but always stayed on his feet. The shield didn't fall and the sword kept on parrying until at last Jalam's fury was spent. Then there came a moment when the two of them simply stopped. They were within a sword's length of each other but neither raised his weapon. The men simply stood there, facing each other, swaying, and it looked for all the world as if nothing but their armour kept them upright. They'd been fighting for twenty-five minutes. The crowd had been cheering and yelling but now they all fell silent.

The silence lengthened. Then there was a clatter. It was Abaddon's shield, dropping from his hand. A roar echoed from inside the big man's helmet and he launched himself in a shoulder charge at Jalam. With perfect timing, Jalam side-stepped and as the giant staggered past him, Jalam swung his elbow into the middle of his back. Abaddon sprawled face down and lay still on the ground.

The cheering went on for a long time, but at last there was silence for Earl Melech as he held up Jalam's hand and pronounced him Grand Champion and Commander of the Army. Jalam took off his helmet and Earl Melech placed a thin circle of gold round the young man's head. But then something totally unexpected happened. Jalam took the gold circlet off and held it up.

'This prize is not for me to wear!' he shouted. 'I claim the title of Champion for a far greater warrior than I could ever be – I claim it for Baladan!'

There was instant uproar and confusion. All the judges gathered and soon a furious argument was raging. Some claimed that if the greatest warrior of the Tournament said there was someone even greater, then they ought to take notice but the others demanded to know how they could possibly make a Champion out of someone who hadn't even turned up to fight?

The judges might have gone on arguing till nightfall but suddenly a warning roar from the crowd made them look towards Jalam. The confusion had lasted long enough for Abaddon to gather his wits and enough strength to heave himself onto his feet behind Jalam's back. Now he had hold of his sword and the judges were just in time to see him bring it crashing down on Jalam's unprotected head. Though it was only a blunted sword, it was enough to shatter the young man's skull. He dropped like a log.

Abaddon seized the fallen circle of gold. He held it high and roared at the crowd: 'Who will you have, Baladan or Abaddon?'

What happened next had obviously been planned well in advance. Suddenly, groups of leather jackets appeared in every section of the crowd. Most contestants had left their weapons in the camp after they'd finished fighting but the leather jackets were all armed and they drew their swords now.

They set up a steady chant of 'Abaddon! Abaddon!' and with the help of their drawn swords, they made sure that everyone else joined in. Then a squadron of Abaddon's riders came galloping into the ring, fully armed, and surrounded the four earls and their councillors. Abaddon walked over to Earl Melech, gave him the gold circle and bowed down before him. Earl Melech was left in no doubt as to what he had to do. He placed the victor's crown on Abaddon's head, raised the robber's hand in his and shouted: 'The people have spoken – the Grand Champion is Abaddon!'

On the mound beyond the battlefield, Baladan wept.

'If you'd been there, it wouldn't have happened!' Ruel accused. 'How could you? How could you let it happen?'

He and Zilla were the only ones who had come back to tell Baladan what had happened to Jalam. The others had been too stunned and sickened to move.

'You'll see him again,' Baladan said quietly.

'Don't be stupid!' Ruel answered. 'He's dead.'

A few minutes later, Ruel saw another figure coming towards the mound. It was Zethar. He had desperately wanted to fight for Abaddon in the Tournament but the robber chief had told him his special job was more important than any amount of fighting. For Zethar to do it, Baladan would have to think Zethar was still part of his group. So all day long, Zethar had been a silent moody presence among the friends. Now his moment for action had come. When he reached the top of the mound, Zethar went up to Baladan and took him on one side. They talked for some time before Baladan came back to Ruel and Zilla.

'Zethar and I have to go on a journey now,' he said. 'We're heading south. Go and tell the others, and if you want to, you can join us. It's time to meet the Great Dragon.'

AUTHOR'S NOTE

I was sitting at home, relaxing one evening towards the end of the week when the phone rang. It was my old friend Michael Taylor. He was just ringing to let me know he'd be coming to hear me preach at the children's service at our church on Sunday.

'Great, see you there,' I said, and put the phone down. Then I put my head in my hands. I'd forgotten it was a children's service, and I'd been busily preparing a sermon for adults all week! I lay down on the settee, closed my eyes, and asked God to send me a story to tell on Sunday – and be quick about it! He did, and that's how the stories in the *Rumours of the King* trilogy got started.

The story I told that Sunday morning was inspired by one of the Bible readings for the day, which was from the Gospel of Mark. Afterwards, I wondered if I could write more about the dragon slayer and his friends using the stories of Jesus as my inspiration. So that's what I did, and I soon found there was enough material to make three books!

Steve Dixon

If you've enjoyed this book, look out for the other two titles in the *Rumours of the King* trilogy.

The story begins in...

Out of the Shadows

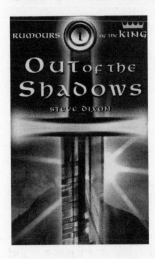

'A horrible feeling, like something squashing his heart, sent Ruel racing towards the forest. He arrived just in time to see two men leading the latest sacrifice up towards the trees. Ruel saw at once what his heart had known already. The victim was Safir.'

The village of Hazar has lived under the shadow of The Reaper for a long time. People are taken and never seen again. But when Ruel's sister is chosen, he decides to find out what happens to the sacrifices; he decides to fight back.

ISBN 1 85999 671 X

How will it end?

The Empty Dragon

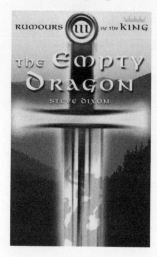

Abaddon is determined to have the whole Kingdom bow before him, but Baladan's followers refuse to go down without a fight...

'The sound of so many people kneeling made a dull rumble, like a wave running up a pebbled beach. But then there was a strange sigh, like the tide ebbing away again. It was the combined gasp of all those who suddenly noticed that something was wrong; when everyone else had knelt, a small group in the outer ring had remained firmly on their feet.'

It's time to take a stand.

Only one can kill the dragon.

Only one can be King.

(published February 2004)

ISBN 1 85999 746 5

You can buy these books at your local Christian bookshop, or online at www.scriptureunion.org.uk/publishing or call Mail Order direct: 08450 706 006